Rest Stops

E G Slade

Keep the work
going!
C Slade

ISBN: 1-4637-2893-X
ISBN-13: 9781463728939

Dedication

This book is dedicated to all the urban public Montessori schools in this country:

- To the many dedicated adults who work daily to touch the lives of children and inspire them without ever knowing the impact of their work.
- To the children and families who place their trust and confidence into a century-old method based on humans' innate love of learning.

And to my family, for their unwavering belief in me and my work in this world.

May it be a better place as a result of our commitment and our faith.

Chapter 1

Home

Where I live is all buildings and sidewalks with junkies on the corner and so much goin on all the time you got to keep your eyes open. Anybody who lives two miles from school has got to walk even if there's snow and it's so cold you can feel your eyelids freezing to your eyeballs. That's the rule in Springfield. One time, when Popi got taken to jail, I cried on the way to school and Edgar tole me to knock it off or I be showing up at school with icicles hanging off a me and that wouldn't look so good. It made me laugh to think a that and so then I didn't cry no more.

Times like that, I'm glad me and Edgar still go to the same school even though he be in eighth grade and I be in fourth. That's the thing about a Montessori school is you can go there when you're just three years old and stay until you be old enough to go to high school. Momi and Popi didn't pick what school for me and Edgar to go to and so we got stuck in Zanetti where all the trouble was, but that turned out to be lucky cause then they made it Montessori to fix all that. Some kids say it was to get white kids to go there because now some do, but I think it was to fix all that trouble. Not that it's all fixed, but things are better.

Today is the first hot day of spring and I gotta walk a different route because we're staying with Uncle Luis for a couple weeks. I thought that'd be real good, but Ramona walks the same way, and she is in some kinda bad mood. She already started up with me on the way and now she is all in my face lining up to go into class. Ms. L talked to her twice already but when she looks the other way Ramona starts bobbing her head with her hand on her hip imitating Ms. L That is all wrong.

I look the other way which makes Ramona real mad and she comes over and pushes up against me. Miss Munoz is walking by and sees her so I don't do nothing back but I look at her real mean like I might. Miss Munoz had me and Ramona last year so she knows trouble when she sees it.

"*Por favor*," Miss Munoz begins, but then she catches herself because Ramona doesn't know Spanish like me. "Ladies, please."

I look down at the ground when I hear her gentle voice. That's when I see Ramona's two different shoes and remember her big lie she tole me on the walk to school. "Nice shoes," is all I need to say to get Ramona's blood boiling.

She comes at me like a punch and pushes me into the wall.

Miss Munoz is right there and she separates us real easy, so Ramona is panting on one side and I'm on the other. Ms. L is on the scene then holding Ramona.

The truth is I don't care about Ramona and all her stupid games. I got bigger things on my mind these days.

"Ms. Jones," a walkie-talkie squawks.

I look down the hall and see Miss Faith Jones coming in her flowy, brown print smock. She wears these real African clothes with all big necklaces and earrings to her shoulders, but I don't think they're as ugly as some. Mostly she never wears bright colors, I notice that.

"Yes," Miss Faith says into the radio.

"What's your location?" the principal's voice asks.

"On the second floor, on my way to the Planning Center," she answers.

Two years ago she made that the new name to her office. I don't know how much planning she does, but now kids don't feel so bad about going to talk to her in there. Between that and letting students call her by her first name, I don't think she's much on the principal's good side.

"Could you come by my office?" The principal's voice comes out too loud and Miss Faith turns down the volume button.

"I'm on my way," she says into the radio. Then she looks over at us across the hall.

"*Buenos días*," she says.

"*Buenos días*," I say looking at the floor again. Then like she's reading my mind she comes over to us.

"Good morning, ladies," she says to me, Ramona, and the teachers.

"Good morning," the teachers answer. Miss Munoz takes that to mean she can leave and go do whatever she come down this hall to do. She smiles right in my face before she leaves though and squeezes my shoulder with one a her love-squeezes.

"Morning Miss Faith," I say back to get rid a the lump that squeeze made in my throat.

Ramona doesn't even look up. Her black skin is looking reddish and her fists are balled up at her side and the whole world can see plain she's wearing two different shoes.

"Is everything all right, Ramona?" Miss Faith asks her.

Ramona looks up with fire in her eyes. "No, everything is not alright. I told Kianna my Mama bought me these spensive shoes that's supposed to look different. That's why they so spensive. And she called me a liar and you know thems fighting words if I ever heard any." Ramona points her boney finger at my chest and I want to snap it right off.

Ms. L gives Miss Faith a what-do-you-want-to-do look, but Miss Faith just smiles at her that she be happy to help.

"What do you say we take a few minutes and work this out in the Planning Center?" Miss Faith asks us.

"Thank you, that would be helpful," Ms. L says.

I start to nod, but then I see the cloud over Ramona is growing thicker.

"I don't wanna go to no Planning Center, I wanna take this to the curb with stupid over there, who can't tell a good pair a shoes when she sees 'em," Ramona says through her clenched teeth.

"Kianna, why don't you and I go to the Planning Center," Miss Faith says to me. Then she turns to Ramona.

"Take your time, and when you feel ready, come on and join us."

Practically before she can even finish Ramona storms off in the direction of the Planning Center calling, "No way I gonna let that baby tell it her way first."

Me and Miss Faith look at each other and I think I prolly wouldn't follow many people into that trouble, but Miss Faith just smiles and gives me the idea that she's gonna take care of it. So we walk down the hall to the office and find Ramona slumped in a chair with her arms crossed tight on her chest. I don't feel like sitting down but when Miss Faith tells me to I pick the chair on the other side of the table from Ramona so she can't reach me or nothing.

Miss Faith is sorting something at her desk and I look over and see she's hung up some new saying on the wall: "Don't give up before the miracle." What could that mean? And why did she hang it up there all decorated on that pretty paper. Miss Faith is always pitching me a new one.

"Ms. Jones?" It's the office calling on her radio.

"Yes?" she answers, holding the talk button down.

"Ms. Sanchez will not be in for the meeting."

"Again?" Miss Faith temporarily forgets we're there, sounding for-real annoyed and running her fingers through her tight black curls. "Did she reschedule?"

There's a pause and then "No," like the office knows this is going to piss her off.

It's a long sigh outa Miss Faith like she's a balloon come untied but then she catches my eye and seems to change where she's going.

"Thank you, I'll be down later to follow up," she says into the radio. Then she picks a seat between us and sits in it, even though it be kid-sized and she is way tall for it. "So, from what I understand there is something going on about your shoes. Is that right, Ramona?" she asks.

Ramona nods. Her lips are pressed together like she's got to concentrate to keep her mouth shut.

Miss Faith turns to me. "Do you want to fill me in on what happened?"

"Well, I just said to her nice shoes and she—" I start to say.

"I did not," Ramona busts in. "I didn't do nothing to you, faggot."

Miss Faith and I sit quiet, letting Ramona's words go round and round the room and land back in her lap. That girl is looking for trouble.

"You just all jealous because my mama actually buys me stuff and your mama—"

Miss Faith stands up between me and Ramona so fast it stops Ramona from saying it. Then she turns and looks down at me all nice and says, "Thanks for coming in so willingly to try and work this out with Ramona, but it seems she isn't ready. I'll come back and check in with you later."

Then she walks me out the door.

"Miss Faith," I say when we are in the hall. "Why does Ramona hate me?"

Miss Faith takes a real long time to answer this, like she's got a whole lot of ideas about it, but then she just says, "She has her reasons to be angry, but she's not angry with you."

"She sure *seems* angry with me," I say.

We are in the hall, which is quiet now that the bell has rung and everyone is in class. Miss Faith puts her hand on my shoulder and lets it sit there. "I heard a teacher give a talk last weekend and he said something that got my attention."

She looks to see that I understand what she just said, and even though I don't I let my eyes say I do because I like how her hand feels and it sounds like it's gonna be a story.

"He said insults are arrows that are launched at us and land at our feet. Then we decide whether to pick them up and stab ourselves with them." She pauses and lets that idea fill up the whole hallway before she asks, "Do you understand that idea?"

I think for a moment, then take a guess. "He's saying we be stabbing ourselves?"

Miss Faith smiles at me. "Yes, when we let other people's words hurt us. He's saying we get to decide if we let the words hurt or not."

I smile back at her but then I remember my crooked tooth, so I hide it with my hand. "Well, then I'm not taking her words to hurt me," I say.

"Good." She squeezes my shoulder. "I'll come get you for mediation when Ramona is ready."

"Ms. Jones?" the principal's voice squawks through the radio, at the same moment she opens the door to Ramona crying.

Miss Faith unclicks the walkie-talkie off a her pants. "I'm sorry I was delayed. I'm with a student."

There is a pause, then the principal says, "See me when you are done."

"Miss Faith?" I say quiet so Ramona won't know I'm seeing her crying. "Can I stay on the bench for a couple minutes?"

Miss Faith thinks about it, I guess deciding if I'm trying to get outa class or not, but then she nods okay. She's been real nice to me since Momi…since we been living with Uncle Luis.

I sit down on the bench and look down the hall at our old room with Miss Munoz. I wonder if she's back in there yet or if she'll pass by and say hi on her way back. Then I notice if I turn my head a little more I can see into the Planning Center. Miss Faith is sitting next to Ramona with one hand on her back and just leaving it there while Ramona cries.

Out the window I see cracks of blue sky between the clouds. A pigeon roosts on the windowsill and stands there like it's watching them.

"Ramona," Miss Faith says in a whisper. "Look up very slowly."

And Ramona, who never does what anyone tells her to do, lifts her head real slow.

"There," Miss Faith points with her head.

Ramona turns and sees the pigeon on the ledge. "Is it gonna come in?" she asks.

"I don't know. Do you want it too?" Miss Faith asks her.

Ramona turns around to see if she's serious and the pigeon startles and flies away. Ramona looks quickly back to the window. "Aw, I'm sorry Miss."

"It's all right. I have a feeling she'll be back," Miss Faith says.

"Why'd ya say that?" Ramona asks. "And how do you know it's a girl." Her face still has tears all on it and her hair got loose from its tight braids and is frizzy all around her face.

"That's an excellent question. How can you tell the difference between a male and a female pigeon?" Miss Faith asks her.

"Don't know," she says.

"Do you want to find out?"

"Yeah," Ramona says.

I can't believe they're talking junk like this about no pigeon. What about her pushing me in the hall? What about her stupid shoes?

Miss Faith gets up and goes over to her phone, pushing the buttons and looking out the window at the city where the bird flew off. "Theresa? This is Faith up in the Planning Center. I'm wondering if you have any bird books that might have information about pigeons."

Ramona is watching her on the phone and Miss Faith puts her thumb up like there's a book down there.

"Okay great. I have a student here, Ramona, who would like to do some research on pigeons. Can I send her down?"

It musta been a yes cause she hangs up and Ramona stands up to go.

"Before you go, Ramona, I wanted to tell you that the nurse just put a note in my box yesterday saying she has too many shoes in her office and she'd be grateful if I knew anyone who could take a pair or two away. I wonder if you'd be willing?" Miss Faith says this not looking at Ramona, but feeling around her desk like she lost something.

Ramona stands real still and even though her back is to the door I can feel her bad mood pressing out.

"Well, I don't know, I just got this fancy new pair," she says all casual like.

"I was thinking if you want to keep them for special occasions you could help the nurse out and just take a pair for around school. A pair you don't care about getting scuffed up. You could stop on your way to the library."

I think by now Ramona's got to know Miss Faith's game, and I be waiting for the lightning to start cracking. But then another miracle happens and Ramona bobs her head in a half nod, half swagger.

"Miss Jones?" the radio asks. "What's your location?"

"That's a good idea Miss. I'll keep these ones for special," Ramona says.

"Should I call the nurse and tell her to expect you?"

She nods again saying nothing.

"Before you go, I'm wondering how we should take care of the business with Kianna?"

I sit up real straight when Miss Faith says this. I look the other way so I can't see them, but I can still hear what they say.

"Aw, that weren't nothing," Ramona says.

There's a quiet and I'm guessing Miss Faith's trying to figure out if I'll be too mad Ramona didn't get in no trouble for pushing me. I think maybe I don't care neither.

"Would you be willing to make things right with her then? Say, when you get back from the library?" Miss Faith asks.

Maybe Ramona nods at that because there's nothing said and then Miss Faith says, "Maybe she'd like to do the pigeon research with you?"

"Yeah! She would I bet. Kianna loves animals."

"Miss Jones? Your location?" the radio asks again.

"I'm in the Planning Center," Miss Faith says into the radio.

"Can you go to room 107?"

That's my brother's class. I hope he didn't do nothing stupid. We only got six more days of school here.

"I need to make two calls and then I'm on my way," Miss Faith says into the radio. She musta forgot about the principal wanting to see her. "Ramona, Kianna is just outside on the bench. Why don't you see if you can get things straight with her before you go downstairs."

I look real interested in my nails when she comes out the door.

"Hey," Ramona says tough but friendly.

"Hey," I say like I couldn't care less.

"Wanna study pigeons?"

I shrug like I could take it or leave it.

"There was one in the office there," she says.

I look at her like I don't believe it, even though I saw it too.

"For real!" She starts to get worked up. "You can even ask Miss Faith!"

"Okay," I say to calm her down.

"Okay about the pigeon in the office? Or okay to the research?" she asks.

"Okay to both." I smile at her. "Okay I'm not mad you pushed me." I think she might ignore the last part, but then she smiles real big. Her teeth are so white next to her black skin and so straight. I put my hand up over my mouth when I smile back at her.

I want to smile like that, real big and true. It was hard before, but now I gotta just hope I'll ever smile like that one day. That's what I want.

Chapter 2
Home

It's eight forty-five and already she's on my case. It ain't my fault this school has babies going here, but they gonna learn the street one way o another. Might as well be me in the hall they hear it from.

"Edgar," Miss Colon calls me to her door and talks to me in Spanish, but it's too late. The narc teacher already called the office on me. She's got it out for me that whitey and Colon knows it. She be stuck in all the school business so she can't say nothing but I know she sees how it's always the spic kids get turned in for stuff.

I don't care anymore anyway. Six days I be jetting this place—what're they gonna do to me today?

I look down the hall and what if it isn't Miss J coming. I turn and face the wall. She makes me talk about "feelings" and her voice is so kind I want to squeeze her till it hurts.

Even though I'm facing the wall, and the two of them don't say nothing, I can feel Miss Colon looking at Miss J and everything that means. They're both totally screwed up thinking I gonna make something of myself or some juice like that. Can't they see it's a lost cause?

Jaquan cruises in just in time. The boy be my comic relief with a temper.

"Jaquan, where's your late pass?" Miss Colon asks sternly. He supposed to be in her class so she's in charge a him, unlike me who's the property of across the hall for the first class anyway.

I turn then cause I don't want to miss the show. He does this act where he's feeling all his pockets like it's there somewhere with this big grin on his face so you know he's messing.

"Office," Miss Colon says.

My boy looks shocked like he can't believe her. Miss J smiles at him and yanks her thumb towards the office and he goes off down the hall talking at them pretend-pissed-off the whole way till the double doors at the other end.

"Ms. Jones? What's your location?" The principal sounds bent.

Miss J takes a big breath and lets it out before she clicks her radio and answers. "I'm in Middle School."

"I expected you in my office…." It sounds like the principal wants to say more but she leaves it at that.

Miss J looks at me and I know she wants me to come with her to the Planning Center to wait while she goes next door to the principal. On a bad day I'd act like I didn't know this, but today it ought to get me outa class for the resta whitey's rant. I'll take it. That's what I want—to get outa this. I nod real slight. Miss Jones smiles slight back.

"I'll be right there," she says into the radio and without a word even to Miss Colon we be walking down the hall to the stairs. She knows Colon gonna tell whitey the office got me. We got this routine all figured.

I follow her but walk a ways behind. When we get to the principal's office she signals for me to sit on the bench there in the hall. I sit down with a thud. Miss J goes into the office and I just sit there like litter. Thing is I want to matter. That's what I want.

Chapter 3
Home

I'm a man of routines. I like to get up, shower, dress, eat breakfast, put on my shoes at the door, and leave at the same time every morning. I'm on a mission to take good care of myself, to do a better job of living each day with meaning. I had taken a wrong turn and been lost in self-loathing, but now I'm on a new kick of self-actualization. Part of that is letting myself wear more colors, especially soft pinks and easy yellows, which I love but never let myself have before.

I live in the Quadrangle and it takes precisely sixteen minutes to walk to my office at the accounting firm on State Street. That gives me four extra minutes in case of bad weather, but I enjoy having them leftover so I can hang up my coat, and put my lunch in the office fridge before anyone else does.

I eat my bologna sandwich at noon just as the church bells on Howard Street are chiming. Often, but not always, I picture the kids next door to that church at the Zanetti school eating their school lunch.

At three fifty-five I log off my computer and straighten my desk for the next day, so that at four o'clock I can be in my coat walking back out the door. This has been my routine for the past two years and ten months, since I finished night school and my sponsor recommended me for this job. He's the one that showed me how important routines are in staying clean and sober and I'm grateful. If I hadn't taken his advice I wouldn't be able to help get the kids out of Springfield and down to Florida. Because of routines I have a nest egg to use and time off from work saved up. I haven't missed one day in two years and ten months. Now I have 12 days saved up, which should be more than enough to travel the 1,432.95 miles to Florida, stay for a day or two and then travel the 1,432.95 miles back home to Springfield. According to MapQuest the trip there should take 23 hours and 15 minutes, but I imagine with Kianna and Edgar along it may take an hour or two longer than that. They aren't very efficient. Edgar wears his pants so low he can't walk very fast and Kianna takes forever because she is curious about everything. This isn't a bad quality in and of itself, but most times the questions wear on me after a fairly short amount of time.

Luckily my new meditation tapes have arrived mail order—twelve in the box set, lasting twenty-four hours in total time. That means they would last the whole way to Miami and possibly subdue some of the questions.

I've been saving them in my bottom drawer so that I won't start listening until the trip begins. This is another part of taking care of myself; having things to look forward to. Last month I didn't eat out once, put the money in a pickle jar and then checked into the Marriott for one night. It was luxurious. I brought my bathing suit and did laps in the pool. They were renovating the hot tub, but I took a long soak in my room afterwards and then put on my favorite pink button-up with a lovely silk tie from an old flame and ate in the hotel dining room as though I were from out of town. The Marriott is a block from my work.

These small steps I'm taking to feel better and treat myself like I deserve it are helping. Last night I had the most peaceful dream about looking up at the stars and seeing pictures there. I woke up with such a wonderful feeling, until I remembered what happened. Even so, all day I had a sense of rightness in the world and that has to be worth something given everything that is going on and how right it isn't.

There are only two days until the trip begins and when I remember that I feel a quickening in my pulse. It's a little rush that I get and then I have to do the deep breathing that I learned at yoga class—in through the nose, out through the mouth. Yesterday it happened while I was at my desk at work and after a few rounds I noticed Myra, the office assistant, staring at me so I stopped. That's when I learned that even a few breaths can really help.

Maybe all this worrying is for nothing. Maybe the trip will be wonderfully easy, and the kids will enjoy it. I said this at a meeting last night and Carl said low, but so everyone could hear him, "Denial is more than a river in Egypt," and people laughed. That hurt my feelings but I acted like I didn't hear him and finished with the Serenity Prayer to remind everyone the purpose of the meetings. Then they all said "Thanks Luis" in unison and it was the next person's turn to share.

I don't know how I'll get to meetings on the trip. But then it won't be that long, and I'll be home for the main weekly meeting. See there—I'm worrying again without reason, borrowing trouble as Jackson would always say. He bought me the silk tie and the first time I held it I started to cry a little thinking about the first stain it would have. It was so perfect and refined I couldn't help worrying just a little.

The thing is there are so many pieces I can't control. I can get it just right—get up on time, showered and into freshly pressed pants and a minute after I'm on the street a bus could come by and change all that. Right here, right now I am asking the Universe for help and guidance dealing with life's uncertainties. That's what I want.

Chapter 4
Massachusetts

When Edgar stood in the door and told me she was dead I didn't believe him for a second. He's all the time telling me junk so I said, "Get out!" and threw a rolled up pair of dirty knee-highs at him. But that day Edgar just stood there like he's younger instead of older, pulling at his fake gold chains, letting his finger glide this way and that along the curve of them.

He stood there a good long time before he says my name, "Kianna," like he's going to say something else, but then he just said it again, "That's it. Momi is dead." And then I thought he was going to cry, but he left before that happened. I was half thinking he was still messing with me, but all a sudden I thought *what's gonna happen to us now?* And I jumped up off the bed and followed Edgar.

I heard banging in the hall and I knew Mrs. Perez had her big black pan out again and she was whacking the wall with it to make the dealers run off, only they're so used to her they don't run anymore.

"Get outa here, I gonna call the police!" She hollered. That might be the only sentence she knows in English.

"Edgar, wait up," I said as I seen him going out the door. "What do you mean? What happened to Momi?"

But he let the door slam behind him and by the time I got it open again the hall was empty.

I waited a long time that day for anyone to come by. Edgar told me after school and it was way after dark before I heard a knock on the door.

"Who's that?" I said, making my voice sound grown up and serious, but then I heard Uncle Luis's voice and I ran to let him in.

⊙⊙

Now we're on this stupid trip that Uncle Luis keeps calling a road trip like it's some kinda holiday. Really he's taking us to Miami to get rid of us. He don't want no kids because he's a fag. That's what Edgar says. Me, I don't know what having kids and being gay have against each other, but there hasn't been a good time to ask this question yet.

I'm sitting here in this red hot car at this rest stop waiting for them to get done with what they're doing so we can get moving. It is only May, but it is hot out here on all this blacktop in the parking lot and the red seats is making it feel even hotter.

Edgar, he's off behind the rest stop smoking. I seen him go out the back door when Luis was in the can. "Where's your brother?" he asked me and I just shrugged like I'm a stupid little kid. Nobody expects much of a fourth grader. I was going to be done being a fourth grader in a couple weeks when school lets out.

Now that I'm missing the last part I think they might make me do the grade over again in Miami. I tole Luis that, that he should wait to do the trip till school's out, it's not that long, but he said, "Naw, we going now before it's too hot." Really what he said sounded better than that because he's an educated man who's making something of his self, at least that's what Momi used to say on the phone to Abuela. Momi and Uncle Luis were always sticking up for each other.

Maybe that's why I can't believe Luis is going through with it and taking us down there to rot. We been living in Springfield as long as I can remember. We haven't even been back to Puerto Rico once in my whole life. That's where Popi is from. Not Edgar's Popi, just mine. We came at different times. Me, I just took a decade. I like that word decade, because it sounds so big and important. Plus Edgar don't know what it means so every time I say it he gets confused looking, like he's got to pretend he knows what I'm talking about. Edgar's not stupid, he just missed a lot of school. Partly he's skipping because I told him I won't do his homework no more unless he pays me and he said "I ain't paying no little git. You do it because I tell you." But in the end he's never able to hurt me no matter what his big talk's all about. I put out my hand, but when he reached in his pocket there was nothing there.

Later I feel real bad when I hear Mrs. Perez banging her pot and I look out the window and see Edgar talking with those dealers. I don't want my brother selling just so he can buy his homework off me. After that night I take it back and tell him it's alright, he can pay me later; I need the extra work to keep me out of trouble. He never does pay me for it, but sometimes after that I find the papers on his floor and I know he's walking with me, but then skipping out and not doing school anymore. That's how it's my fault that Edgar's become a drug dealer.

Now here he comes over to the car with his red blood eyes and that stupid smile.

"Hey angel, what you thinking on?" I'm too old to be called angel now, but when Edgar says it I feel like Momi's right here. My eyes sting and I look away.

"Shut up Edgar," I say like it's all his fault.

"Those some big words outa the little miss," he says pulling open the creaky red door and sitting on the hot front seat.

He smells bad and I feel stuck in here now that he's come, so I pull my door handle and let the door swing open.

"Hey, where you going?" Edgar asks swiveling his head around.

"What's it to you?" I say, still acting tough.

He pretends not to hear and puts on his headphones like he could care less. Well, I could care less. I am sick of Edgar. Sick of this trip and this is only our first rest stop out of town. I go up to the bathroom area, because it's the only thing around and Uncle Luis is nowhere to be seen.

The silver door handle feels cool in my hand and when I pull it open I feel the air-conditioning on my hot skin. I like air-conditioning. It's just plain wrong to be driving so far in a car without air-conditioning. Luis tries to tell us something about how it's bad for the environment, but this heat is bad for my environment. Maybe I'll just live here at this rest stop. It's a nice enough room with some maps in pockets on the wall and a couple of machines I could eat out of with bathrooms just down the hall.

There's a big picture hanging on the wall and I sit in one of the cool plastic chairs and just stare at it. It's black and white and of the beach. Some big dark clouds are hanging over the ocean with just this one spot where maybe if it's strong enough the sun could bust on through and brighten things up a bit. Only I don't think that's going to happen anytime soon. I think those waves are coming in one after the other and the sky isn't going to be able to see a thing with all those clouds in the way. But then what do I know. I've never even seen a real beach before.

"Kianna." That's Luis calling from the door like I'm going to jump up and run right over there.

"Kianna!" he says again like I'm deaf. I look straight ahead at all that foam in the water. I know he's gonna come and sit, because what else is the man going to do? Leave without me? Let him. I'll live here like I said in all this air conditioning.

Uncle Luis settles into the stiff orange seat connected by bars to mine. "I just have three words that I want to say," he starts, but then he doesn't say them. Did he go and get high with Edgar? What happens to Edgar when he goes smoking is he can't remember what he was talking about. Sometimes he just flat stops talking and that's the end of it. This one time a couple weeks ago, after we found out about Momi, a social worker had come to make us move in with Uncle Luis and we were sitting around on the couch for the last time. Uncle Luis went in the kitchen and Edgar had gone out on the fire escape before the worker had even left the building. I was feeling scared that she'd look up and see him smoking and then I'd lose the only one I got left. But she didn't and soon here comes Edgar smelling like that Indian man across the hall. He lights all kinda stuff and the hall reeks of it. Anyway we was sitting there, waiting for Uncle Luis to finish packing up stuff in the kitchen and Edgar starts talking all about Momi and then right in the middle of a sentence he just stops. I'm sitting there pretty interested in what he's talking at me, so I say, "What? What Edgar?" And I try to be patient and wait but he doesn't say nothing. "Eddie?" I try to get him with nicknames he hates. "Gar gar?" That second one is what I first called him when I was learning to talk. But still he's so stoned or so stubborn that he just sits there staring. I'm trying to remember what he was saying when he stopped talking. Something about before Popi came when it was just he and Momi, but I can't quite remember what he didn't want to say. When I was a baby? Something.

"Time to go," Luis's voice breaks through my thinking like bus brakes at your stop.

I don't want to leave my thoughts, my plastic chair, my ocean. I don't want to leave this cool room and go back out into the heat.

"It's too hot," I say.

"Yes it is." And I like that Luis doesn't try to argue with me. He gets up and reaches for my hand. His rings shine in the light and his shirt collar is lopsided. I take his smooth hand and let him pull me up. I straighten his collar and he smiles at me. "It's going to be okay," he says in a soft voice.

I am suddenly angry. I want to spit in his face. Instead I turn back to the ocean on the wall, look for the last minute into the waves, before I stomp out of there to the hot car.

Luis follows me without saying anything or trying to catch up. But I can feel him back there, his shiny shoes squeaking and the little humming noise he makes. I admit I've liked that humming noise in the past but just now it is like the TV station gone off the air and it makes my head fill with fuzz.

I get into the car and slam the door so Edgar will know I'm back even though he is slumped down with his eyes closed and his headphones on. Uncle Luis gets in his side and starts up the engine. His car is just like him; it's odd with its own humming noise. He puts it in reverse and we back out of there and head onto the highway.

I like the highway because it is so fast. I put my head out the window and the air blows my hair everywhere, but then I pull it back off my face to show it where to go and it stays there, blowing behind me like a black coat.

My mother had a long black coat like that. She got it from Popi one time he won a scratch ticket. They were so happy that night with candles lit up on the table and a roast pig. Momi was so excited she wore that coat to dinner acting like she was royal, swinging it all around. Popi told her, "Enough already, it's nothing," but she was so happy she couldn't stop it. She was in a mood, calling Edgar "Eddie," which he hates but that night he let her do it. I remember having to rub my cheeks in bed because they weren't used to smiling so hard.

Later on in the night though I startled awake hearing their mad voices on each other like dogs in the alley. For a long time I didn't understand why it had to be like that, why they yelled at each other. Then Popi musta got so mad he smacked her and I could hear her head hit the other side of the wall from where I sat up in bed. My heart stopped and I held my breath listening. I thought I was going to hear her crying then, but instead she scared me bad with this long scream. When I heard a thump I pictured Popi hitting the floor and then there was crash of something breaking and I figured she must have jumped on him. I pictured blood across his face where her nails scratched him, little dots at first and then gushes like when Leanexa and Roxie fought that day. I leaned my ear to the wall just as Momi cried out in pain and suddenly I was up and running out my door to get to her.

Just then their door flew open and out rushed Popi. They didn't say another single word to each other. Popi went down the hall past me and then the door slammed loud and echoing. Then the apartment went spooky quiet. The dark was so big I couldn't see Momi from the door. I heard Edgar behind me. When I felt his hands on my shoulders I jumped a little not knowing until then how scared I was. On accident I just turned and hid in Edgar's front. He put his arms around me and let me be there for a minute. Then he moved me aside and went into Momi and Popi's bedroom.

I saw the light come pouring out the door and I knew Edgar had gone right to the metal lamp on the low table by their mattress and switched it on. He didn't say anything but I was thinking *Momi is dead* and I was too scared to look in there.

"Get a towel." Edgar's voice took control of me and I did what he said. When I got back with the towel I almost couldn't take it in the room, but then Edgar said real quiet like he knew my problem, "Bring it here Kia." So I went in and handed it to him.

Momi was not dead. She was looking up at me so scary I looked away to Edgar. He wrapped the towel around her arm where blood was coming out. Popi had stabbed her with something. My eyes wandered, so I didn't have to look at Momi's face or the towel where the blood started to soak through. I saw that the picture of our family posed in the Sears studio was on the floor, still in its shiny frame but the glass was all broken. I thought: *Popi stabbed Momi with a piece of the glass from our family picture* and that is when I started to cry. I did it without making a sound so Edgar couldn't tell me to shut up, but still I cried.

It makes me sad to think of that night now. To see Momi in my mind, bleeding, looking so gone. And now she is gone and I have to leave my Springfield apartment and move to Miami.

"What'cha thinking back there?" Uncle Luis always sounds so cheerful and I wonder what it could be that makes him happy. Maybe he has a boyfriend and he's *in love.*

"You got a boyfriend?" I blurt out.

"What's that?" he asks like he didn't hear me right, or maybe he thinks I won't say it again.

"A boyfriend. You got one?"

He doesn't answer. Then he says, "Entering Connecticut!" like it's not the very next state over.

I lean forward over the seat. "I said, you got a boyfriend?" Then I don't give him a chance not to answer again. "You think I don't know you are *pato?* Well, I've known a long time so you can get over it and just tell me. You got a boyfriend or not?"

"Not," he says after a moment.

"Too bad."

"Yeah," he says, staring ahead at the highway.

"What happened to the last one?"

"What last one?" He is playing games with me now.

"What was that guy's name, from Forest Park? The black guy with the big bald head?" I want to shake his shoulder, but I don't. Edgar is still slumped down with his eyes closed. His rap music is playing so loud that I can hear it clearly, but I think Edgar is asleep. "Jackson! That was his name. What happened to Jackson?"

"Jackson?" he says, sounding surprised, or like he's playing dumb, or both.

"Yeah? Or wasn't he your last one?"

Maybe the idea that I might make him say more gets him going. "How do you know Jackson?"

"I met Jackson last Halloween when he answered the door at your apartment, and what are you so afraid about being gay for?" Only I'm sorry I say this last part because I know exactly why he's afraid about being gay. I look at the scar on the side of his neck facing me and I remember the night Momi went to get him after they cut him.

It was another time when I was supposed to be sleeping only the phone woke me up and then the sound of Momi and Popi arguing. Popi was saying in Spanish, "You will not go out at this time of night."

I couldn't hear Momi real well because she must have been in the bathroom, but then Popi answers her, "You will not because I said so!"

Then I hear Momi's feet coming stomping and she says in her low but I-mean-it voice, "He's my brother and I am not leaving him on the street."

Then Popi says, "You been fending for your faggot *hijo* all these years," and I hear the slap and imagine her face on fire as she dares him to say more. Then it's quiet until the door shuts behind her. I lay awake for a long time wondering what happened to Uncle Luis and if Popi was going to let him in when they come back, but then I must have fallen asleep because the next thing I hear is water running like for a bath and Momi is talking real sweet to Popi and their voices are low so I can't hear the words, but I know it's going to be alright.

The next morning when I went out for school, Uncle Luis was asleep on the couch and I saw a big bandage on his neck. He looked real skinny lying like that with just a small blanket over him. I went past real quiet.

Edgar told me the whole gay-bashing thing on the way to school and the next time after that when I seen

Uncle Luis, I didn't feel so mad at him anymore for be-ing *pato.*

"Are you wearing your seat belt?" he asks me now.

"What do you think?" I answer.

"I think you should sit back and put your seat belt on."

"Why? Afraid you're going to crash us?" And even before I'm done saying it I want to take it back. I don't mean to give Uncle Luis a hard time about everything; it just comes out sounding like I do. To make up for it I slide back in my seat and click the seat belt as loud as I can so he knows I'm doing what he said.

I lean my head up against the side of the door and watch the clouds. They look so close really, like if I reached out the open window, or maybe if I stood on the roof of the car anyway, I might just touch that real, big fluffy one. This makes some time go by picturing myself going down the highway on top of the car pulling a cloud along behind me, and me with a big smile on my face for all of Connecticut to see.

Luis leans forward and pushes a cassette tape into the player. A man's voice with a funny accent comes into the car. The speaker on my door is the only one that works so it is coming out real loud. "*Relax now, and still your mind….*"

"What is this?" I say, only Uncle Luis can't hear me over the tape.

In his funny accent, the man through the speaker is saying there is no point in learning more things. Learn-ing is for your mind. Knowledge is for your mind. Well, duh knowledge is for your mind, what does he think it's for? "*It is through stillness that one finds true wisdom.*"

This makes me stop right there. So he's saying knowledge and wisdom are different? I wish I could ask Miss Faith about this one. Miss Faith is a good person to ask questions no one else will answer.

"*Close your eyes. Find stillness.*" I sure hope Uncle Luis is not closing his eyes. I lean forward enough to see he's not, so I sit back. I have nothing else to do so I close my eyes. I try to sit real still, but as soon as my eyes are closed, I feel how my bare legs are sticking to the seat and it feels itchy. I unstick them, but when I put them back down they stick again. I open my eyes and look around the backseat for something to put under my legs. I see Uncle Luis's sweater on the seat. I lean over and feel it. It is so soft, I swear I have never felt a sweater this soft. I pull it to my face and rub it there. God that is a soft sweater. I am so hot and still I can't stop touching this sweater. The man is going on without me so I stick the sweater between the red seat and my legs and close my eyes to catch up.

"*Feel what you feel. Let your mind loose.*" I feel like I am sitting on that cloud I was touching a couple minutes ago. My mind pictures that now. I actually feel pretty happy doing this. I don't know about wisdom, but it's pretty fun.

"What is this?" Edgar's harsh voice rips into my cloud. The man's voice stops and I hear the tape pop out up front. Edgar takes it and throws it out the window. I jump, like I am going to catch it, like it's something precious to me.

"Edgar!" I yell.

Uncle Luis swerves over into the breakdown lane and comes to a careful but kinda fast stop.

"What're you gonna do? Make me walk back and get it?" Edgar says.

Uncle Luis says nothing, but he nods his head matter-of-factly. This is how Miss Faith is with the kids at school. She just acts like they are going to do the things she asks and I can't believe it but they almost always do. There was that one time Tyrone threw that chair at her, but I heard later he was all drugged up when he did it.

"Yeah right," Edgar says in a mean way and he slumps back down with his headphones again.

I open the door to get out and go back for it myself.

"Kianna." That's all, just that one word, my name, that's all Uncle Luis says, but I know what he is telling me. I close the door. It's so hot just sitting still. Out the window I see a Taco Bell bag and an old shoe. What do those things have to do with each other? How did they end up here on the side of Route 91 as litter? I start to make the story up in my head but I get too hot and can't finish.

Uncle Luis opens the door and gets out. I think he is giving up, that he's going back for the tape, but I am wrong. He begins doing some weird stretching business right on the side of the road! God I hope none of my friends are going to Hartford for anything today. I slump down in my seat.

At that Edgar slides up. We are horses on the carousel at the Holyoke Children's Museum. "What the…?" Edgar is pointing at Uncle Luis who is standing outside the car, balanced on one foot with the other flat against his knee and both hands together above his head. He is still as a statue. The only thing moving is his hair from a semi that blasts by. I think it's pretty good, but Edgar throws his headphones on the car floor and without a word he gets out, slams the door and begins lumbering down the highway. I watch him out the back window with his jeans falling off his butt and his wife beater tee shirt tight on his back.

I figure it's safe for me to get out now, so I do. I sit on a little patch of grass behind the shoe. It looks like it's been here a pretty long time. Maybe when it rains little mice come out and live in it. The laces look pretty chewed up.

Just when I think I might faint from heat and total boredom, I see Edgar's figure coming back up the highway. I look over at Uncle Luis who is sitting beside me now with his legs crossed, staring at the cars going by without really seeing them I think. He hasn't said more than a single word since asking about my seat belt. I look back and Edgar is closer now so I can see the mad on his face.

I know it will make things worse if I watch him come so I look out across the traffic myself. I pretend the cars are like one of those pictures you stare at a long time and then you see something else is there. Only I don't see anything in all those cars.

Edgar throws the tape in the dirt near the Taco Bell bag and gets in the car. Uncle Luis smoothly picks it up as he stands and puts it in his pocket. He offers me a hand up.

"Rest stop over, kiddo." Seriously, who says kiddo? But I give him my hand and let him pull me up. I learned a long time ago that saying nothing when people are angry is the way to go; eventually everybody gets over it.

It was so quiet in the car after that I must have fell asleep because the next thing I know the car is stopping and I have to pee. I look out the window at the people and they're mostly white so I figure we must still be in Connecticut.

"You hungry?" Uncle Luis asks and I nod.

We get out the car and begin to walk toward the rest stop when I see Edgar isn't coming. I go back to the car and look at him slumped down like a pile of rags in the seat. He has on his sunglasses but I can see his eyes are closed. I reach in the open window and push his shoulder.

"Wake up," I demand.

He doesn't move. I shake him. "Edgar! Wake up!"

Still he doesn't move and I look across the parking area at Uncle Luis who stands there with his hands in his pants pockets looking up at the sky. I think Edgar might be dead and Uncle Luis is daydreaming over there.

I shake him harder. "I swear I will kill you if you are dead!"

Edgar pushes my hand off him and growls at me.

I am so mad he scared me like that that I throw open his door and demand he get out. He looks a little surprised but he doesn't move. His sunglasses are tilted and he seems ridiculous. I am so mad at him for looking stupid like that.

"Edgar Juan Santiago, get out of that car this minute!" I make my voice sound like Momi's and I think it's pretty close.

To my surprise Edgar laughs. He does, he laughs and gets out of the car. I make my face look satisfied but really I feel confused. Not because Edgar laughed at me for shouting at him in the parking lot, but because his laugh didn't sound at all familiar. As we all walk into the rest stop, I try to think of when I heard Edgar laugh before that, but we are seated at a table with our food on trays and I still can't come up with a time.

"How come you don't laugh no more?" I ask him right straight out. He is drinking his Coke and he pretends not to hear me. "How come Edgar?"

"How come what?"

"How come you don't never laugh?

"That's a stupid question," he says, lifting his burrito to his mouth and letting the insides slide out on his plate.

"That's what you say when you don't have no answer."

It worries me that Edgar doesn't snap back at this. He just sits there jawing his food. I think my brother is slowly dying.

"How's your food?" Uncle Luis asks.

"I hate Taco Bell," I say. "It belongs on the side of the road."

"Why didn't you pick McDonald's then?" he asks. I must have been thinking about Edgar then and missed the choice. I do like those super skinny fries they have there.

"Nothing good there either," I complain. I decide then and there—I'm gonna be a pain-in-the-butt. I throw my taco down like it is garbage. "I'm not eating this shit."

Uncle Luis looks at me over his drink, but he doesn't say anything. It's Edgar who says, "Watch your mouth."

"I will not," I snap back at him, "And you can't make me." I cross my arms so he gets I'm serious.

Edgar just chews his gooey food and says nothing.

I think I might lose him, so I say quickly, "See, you can't make me do it."

Edgar's hand is so fast that I don't see it coming but I feel the sting on my face. I feel crazy mad and I leap across the table at him spilling both our drinks. "You can't tell me what to do. You're not Momi." I get his cheeks with my nails and go to dig in but Edgar jumps up out of his chair and shakes Coke off his hands. He stares at me fierce. I stare back.

Uncle Luis is going nuts, mopping up the table and saying stupid stuff like "whoa there" and "easy now" like we a bunch of horses on TV. Then Edgar turns his back and starts to walk away. I can't take this so I run and jump on his back like a mud wrestler. Out of the corner of my eye I see Uncle Luis coming to get me but before he can, and in one move, Edgar shakes me off and I land on the floor at Uncle Luis's feet. This is more humiliation than I can stand so I leap up and run into the ladies' room by the door.

I go into the last stall and lock it. I sit down with my pants on and pull my feet up onto the seat so my knees are hiding my face. I feel red. I want to cry but there are no tears there to cool me down. I am like a pizza oven, ready to burn up the long wooden paddle they stick in there.

I hate this day. I hate this trip. I hate rest stops.

Chapter 5
Connecticut

When I got the call that Callie was dead, I didn't believe it. I shook my head like I had heard wrong or there was some mistake. I made her say it more than once. Drug overdose around midnight, no identification, nothing except my card and a book of food stamps. All the way to Baystate Hospital I kept thinking maybe it was some other middle-aged Hispanic woman with brown hair and a birthmark on her right shoulder. I don't know that many women and I don't know any of them well enough to know if they have birthmarks. It was possible one of them picked up my card and died of a drug overdose at midnight. Not Callie, not my sister. Please. I was begging.

I'm not what you call a religious man, but in the last ten years or so I have become a spiritual person. I believe in something. I believe in a Higher Power. I know that sounds very AA, and that is where I started my spiritual journey, but it's more than that now. It's more than staying sober; it's a life choice. I choose to be a man of faith, to believe things happen for a reason.

This is what I told myself to keep from begging on the way to the hospital to claim my sister's body after a drug overdose at thirty-four years old. Losing my sister means losing a part of my life I will never have again. Ever.

When I saw her body on the gurney I felt my blood run cold. Her face looked so old and worn, though she is the same age I am. She had a bunch of broken blood vessels around her eyes, and her hair was all dirty and matted. She looked like a stranger, a bum, like someone no one cared for, who no longer cared for herself. How did it come to this? I keep asking this question but it gets me nowhere. I want to think that if I'd known how bad things were that I would have done something, but really what would I have done? Hidden her needles? Flushed her stash? Bought her new shoes? None of that would have made any difference. I am learning that people make their own choices in this life; I cannot stop them. This is part of turning it over, not checking other people's inventories, only my own. The result of this thinking was that I hadn't checked on Callie, hadn't seen her in weeks.

After I identified her body I sat in the bright lights of the hospital, numb to the truth of it. I sent myself into exile for a few hours. But it turns out a self in exile is still a self.

I sat like that until dawn. I have always been afraid of the dark and seeing my sister dead is just the kind of thing that makes me sure I will never go out in the dark again. What was the rush anyway? Edgar and Kianna were both used to getting up and having their mother gone. They were old enough to get themselves off to school. One more day of school before learning their mother was dead hardly seemed like a bad thing.

I remember wanting to call Jackson then. I wanted him to come and put his arms around me, so I could cry, so I could be as weak as I felt. Instead I sat there stiffly until light began to come into the sky. Then I got up and walked out into the day.

The automatic front door of the hospital opened in front of me and I could smell the orderlies' cigarettes from where they leaned against the building smoking.

"Goodbye," I said.

One or two of them nodded kindly and I walked away. I hate pity, and yet somehow I have this life where people are always offering it to me, like a leftover for the alley cat.

I walked to the diner on Main Street for coffee. I needed to clear my head and make a plan. Callie was dead and their father, or at least Kianna's father, Juan, was in jail. Kianna and Edgar would need someplace to live and I was the next of kin. The Department of Social Services would likely be calling me to take them. They are in a phase of favoring "kinship care," as they call it, and they asked me last time Callie was in rehab. I said no then and the kids almost got shipped down to Florida to live with their grandmother, but then that counselor over at their school came up with something till Callie could get her act together again. Remembering all this over coffee brought me to realize that was where the kids would have to go now, to Florida, and that I would have to be the one to take them there.

So the first thing I did the morning after my sister died was to take my little savings and go down and buy a used car. When I walked in there was a man with greasy black hair behind a counter that could have used some disinfectant spray. He was on a computer and looked up when the bell over the door jingled. On the wall behind the counter was a poster that read "The search is over" and it wasn't clear from the image if the search was for the car or the woman in the blue string bikini. I looked away feeling oddly embarrassed.

The man stepped forward and introduced himself as Joe. I explained my situation and he scratched his head with a fingernail that looked too long to belong to this man. Then he grabbed a set of keys off of a hook and beckoned for me to follow him.

A shiny Chevrolet sat at the end of the lot. It was a tidy four door, fire engine red inside and out, a lot of nicks and dents, but not bad on the mileage. He explained that his brother-in-law finished it out on the inside to look like a classic 1945 Chevy because his kid was into the musical *Grease* and her birthday was coming. He stopped there and didn't say the rest of the story. I almost asked him, but having so recently stood over Callie's body in the morgue, I changed my mind.

We haggled over the price and then it was done. I guess I should have looked around and been a more prudent shopper, but it was clean and in good working condition, except for no air conditioning, but after all it's May. How hot could it get?

I feel foolish now, sweating like a track star outside this rest stop waiting for Kianna to come out of the ladies' room. She's not taking all this very well. When I first got over to the apartment, I was all excited to show her the car and I walked in talking. She was sitting alone in the dark apartment and I thought she had gone mute. I guess Edgar had just told her point blank and then took off and left her alone. I knew I shouldn't have told him over the phone, but I was down at the registry of motor vehicles, and the line was awful. I figured they were wondering about their mother by then.

Now that I'm thinking back through it I can see that my anger at Edgar then was more about how stark it was for me to shift gears from where I was, having bought my first car, to where the kids were, and the reality that it was all because their mother was dead. They were both so deadly quiet the next day with the social worker and even through the packing up and loading the car today.

I just don't know a lot about kids. I got some books in the trunk to read at night. There's one Ms. Jones gave me when I came to get the kids. It's written by some Italian woman who invented the school they go to. I guess if you know enough to invent a whole school you must know something about children. She said to start with the part she marked about developmental stages. I wonder what developmental stage has you hide in the rest stop bathroom while your uncle and your brother sweat to death. The other one is something about loss and grief.

"Where you going?" Edgar grunts.

"I'm getting a book out of the trunk. You got anything to read?"

The thug snorts at me and I go around to the back of the car for the book. It is a beautiful day, if it weren't so hot. The sky is so big and mighty without the city filling it up. Maria Montessori. That's her name. That's the kind of school it is, Zanetti Montessori School on Howard Street. She looks awful old to have made that school up. Anyway, it's something to read.

I close the trunk firmly and walk around, but I can't make myself get back in yet. I lean against the car and watch a beautiful man filling his truck tank with gas. His back is so strong in that white tee shirt and his jeans are nice and tight. I like the way he stands while he waits for his tank to fill, so confident and easy. I want to see his face. Maybe he will turn around when he screws in the gas cap. I can wait. The view is good.

I hear Kianna's car door close at the same moment I feel the car shake with her power. She is a little storm. She has been a mighty force right from the beginning. I don't want to get in the hot car with the thug and the storm cloud. I want this man to turn around, notice me, gesture for me to come get in his truck, and then drive off with him to anywhere he's going.

"What's the holdup?" Edgar's voice punctures the idea and I get into the car. I don't want to be in charge of discipline but the whole episode in the Taco Bell cannot be repeated so I turn and face them both.

"That can't happen again," I say.

Edgar goes to put his headphones on but I reach out and stop him. Kianna looks out the window. Her face is hard and sad.

"Look, I know this trip is no joyride for either of you, but you can't just start up hitting and jumping each other in rest stops."

Neither of them says a word, but I know they have heard me.

"Okay?" I ask in a voice just loud enough to be heard.

Kianna watches Edgar to see what he will do. He is staring out the front.

"Okay?" I ask again a little more strongly.

At nearly the same moment I see their heads both nod imperceptibly.

"Okay," I repeat, firm now, like it's a deal. "Buckle up."

If that was a battle, I won. I feel renewed energy and I give a little honk as I pass the man getting into his truck. He is gorgeous. I smile and wave. He looks confused and gets into his truck without waving back.

Back on Interstate 95. Sixty-four miles down, one thousand three hundred seventy-four to go, according to MapQuest. Not that I'm counting. I just set the travel odometer on zero when we left East Columbus Avenue to see how many miles it would be in the end.

We had so many errands to do on the way out of town that we were hot and tired early in the drive. We pulled off 91 for a stretch and drink break before we'd even crossed state lines and then again when Edgar lost his mind and hurled my cassette out the window. I will not stand for that, I will not. I remembered that affirmations tape I had from the library said, "*Treat yourself how you want others to treat you.*" Sure I could have let it go, just one little tape, but I saved up for that set and it was like he'd thrown my hard work out the window. My hard work and everything I believe in. I couldn't let that slide.

I almost started biting my nails on the roadside when Edgar stormed away and didn't come back. I started thinking he had walked back to the last exit and was going to hitchhike a ride back home, or worse get a ride into Hartford and pick up on the streets there. Edgar is a kid just one step from the streets. That counselor sat me down even before this whole thing happened and told it to me straight.

Edgar had been fooling around outside before school and things had gotten out of hand. One of them, I think Jaquan, was touching his hat and Edgar apparently said, "lay off nigger" and then the bell rang and they all went in. Soon after that that Edgar heard Jaquan say something about his mother. That was the last straw; they started hitting each other and the teacher called the Crisis Team. The school policy is that whenever the Crisis Team is called, the students involved are suspended and cannot return until the family has had a meeting with the principal and the school counselor. That was when I got called. Ms. Faith Jones called me at my apartment and asked me if I would come in for Edgar. Apparently Callie hadn't made it in for the meeting. Edgar had already missed too much school waiting for her to come in, so Ms. Jones convinced him to tell her my number. She called me and told me the situation.

I admit I didn't want to get involved at first, but the more I thought of all Callie had done for me the more I knew I had to, so I called my office and told them I was going to be late. Mrs. Van Beckham was due in to have her taxes from last year looked over anyway and I hate doing IRS work. So I went down to the school and met Ms. Faith Jones. The meeting about the fight was pretty standard, but after that she pulled me into her office and told me about Edgar's trouble with reading.

I looked about Ms. Jones's office at the tray with sand and stones on the low table, the painting of a big green field with trees, the book *Peace Begins with Me* propped up and the wind chimes hanging in her window. Then I looked at Ms. Faith Jones. Her curly black hair was growing out and her dark eyes were begging for eye shadow and what was with the African muumuu she was wearing?

"Edgar?" I said, like she must be getting him confused with some boy younger, or dumber.

"Yes," she said, nodding her head.

"Trouble reading?" I asked to be sure I had it right.

"Many children from bilingual homes have difficulty learning to read. The trouble is that Edgar is smart—"

"That's right he's smart so why are you saying he can't read?"

She took a breath, I think more to calm me than to calm herself. "I'm not saying he can't read, I'm saying I think it's a struggle for him. You see, he never wanted to let on that it was hard and so as a result he never received the remedial services he really needed. Now he's beginning to believe the street is the only place for him."

That *did* sound like Edgar, not letting on when things are hard for him. And I had noticed he wasn't around the apartment much these past months when I stopped by there.

"What should we do?" I asked, before I thought through what I was saying.

Her smile widened as she realized she had me.

I had no idea that within a month of that conversation I would be identifying my dead sister, picking up school records, and driving the kids out of town.

Ms. Jones looked so sad that day last week when I stopped by for the records. I went up to her office to say goodbye and that's when she gave me the books. Then she walked me down to the main office.

"When are you taking them?" she asked, handing me the records.

We were in the busy hallway outside the main office. The heat wave wasn't upon us yet and she was wearing yet another long-sleeved, flowing, dark printed outfit.

"Next Tuesday. I can't get time off from my job until then."

"So is Friday their last day or will they be in on Monday?"

I hadn't thought it through that carefully. "Uh, I guess I'll pick them up from here on Tuesday. Around mid-morning?"

Her walkie-talkie buzzed "Ms. Jones, what's your location?"

She held it up to her face. "Outside the main office."

"Call me on the black phone." the voice instructed.

"Okay," she answered. She looked into my eyes earnestly for a long stretch. "Take care," she said, touching me lightly on the arm. And I felt like those two words covered a lot of ground.

"Yeah, you too. And thank you for all your help. And the books. Really." She looked so sad I wanted to rescue her from it. It flashed briefly in my head that we should stay. That I should keep the kids and stay in Springfield, that we could make a go of it. But then her radio buzzed again.

"Ms. Jones? The black phone." And she was gone.

Out of my mouth pops a question about Faith Jones before I can remember that Kianna is in a mood and Edgar is in a punk-boy stupor. Somehow though they pick up on it and begin talking about her schedule and what she does at school. That is until Kianna slam-dunks Edgar and he shrinks back into his shell of his music and his silence. I have this odd feeling of wanting to protect him, but her words are meant to hurt, meant to get him back for hurting her in the Taco Bell, meant to push him away and punish him.

I look over and see that he is gone. I stumble, try anyway. I am babbling, but the conversation about Faith Jones is the first one he's entered. It's my lifeline to Edgar and I can't seem to pull myself in. Edgar slides his headphones over his ears.

I feel irrationally angry with Kianna for this. "Sit back and put on your seat belt!" I snap at her. My eyes lock on the road ahead of me, the flow of traffic, like a row of numbers on an adding-machine tape.

Edgar leans his head back and closes his eyes.

Somehow when I look at him like that I feel all the anger drain from me. I go limp with the weight of it, remembering the first time I saw him as a new baby. I was a different person then strung out on something. The hospital smelled odd and I couldn't stop laughing at the looks on people's faces in the hall, the strange way the light reflected off their skin and made them look lit up like jack-o'-lanterns. That was before I quit the streets and got back into school at night, when my body was my money and I moved from one part of town to another to avoid getting beat up or busted. Another version of self-exile. Another life. So foreign that I shake my head.

I remember the sterile hospital with its bright lights that night was like being on another planet, and I walked delighted and amazed down the halls to Callie's room. But the halls were nothing compared to the sight of Edgar, with his head leaning back and his eyes closed. He was tightly wound up in a little white blanket with bears on it, and his little fists were balled up and resting under his chin. He had a thick patch of black hair in the middle of his head, like one of those psychedelic trolls, and the longest black lashes I had ever seen. He was beautiful.

"Come in here," Callie commanded, waving me over to the bed.

I wanted to, but my feet were stopped by the sight and I couldn't get them going again.

"Come on," she insisted.

"God, Callie, she's beautiful," I made out, and then I started to cry. I didn't want to cry, but between the lights and the baby and my feet not cooperating, I had too much going on to stop the tears.

Callie laughed her burst-out laugh. "It's a boy. His name is Edgar." She looked at me with shining eyes and I saw then all that she had gone through to bring this baby into the world.

"Where is Edgar?" I asked about the father, before thinking it through.

Her face fell and she looked the other way, out the small window between cinder blocks.

"This is the only Edgar now," she said low. Then she fell back to her girlhood habit of fingering the edge of the blanket between her thumb and forefinger.

My feet must have given in at the sight of this because the next thing I knew I was touching her hair. "Never mind, Cal, never mind." I stroked her hair and I remember thinking it felt the way I imagined straw felt, or at least the way straw looked like it felt.

She cried while I stroked her hair, probably thinking about that no-good Edgar and wondering what new woman he was with, until the baby mewed and we both looked at him startled, just then remembering he was there. Edgar always had a way of startling me, right from the beginning.

Those first years of Edgar's life, Callie went clean and actually started a real grown-up life. By the time he was walking, she had an apartment with another mother on Union Street and worked nights at the 7-Eleven so she could be with him during the day. That lasted a pretty long time I think. It's not exactly clear in my mind because those were my loose days and I cannot account for how they passed, until I started to straighten my own life out a little. What I remember about that time was Callie was happy and Edgar was holy. Everywhere that boy went people had to reach out and touch him, like they would be saved or cured or blessed. For a long time Edgar had no sense of his princely status in the neighborhood and his glow was unrivaled.

That all changed when Edgar was four and Callie fell for another bum, Kianna's father Juan. He appealed to her mother's heart coming into the 7-Eleven with a crying baby every morning before she got off. Callie would tell me how he was so lost with what to do with an infant that she had to teach him everything. The first night he came in with Kianna wailing her lungs out, looking for formula. Callie was so thrown off by the newness of the baby and the need in her cry that she went in the back and made up a bottle of formula, just the right temperature and showed him how to feed it to the howling baby. He was so grateful that she had showed him how to make a bottle at the coffee sink. The next morning she took him into the restroom and showed him how to clean and change her right there on the diaper deck. And it went on like that.

I was sleeping on her couch that first week they met and I remember on her night off, her getting up at five in the morning to go down to the 7-Eleven to meet him and take care of Kianna. I honestly don't know if she fell in love with Juan or Kianna, but before long my spot on the couch was gone. I was replaced by Juan and a portacrib.

I didn't mind much though, thinking my sister would be happy and now Edgar would have a sister. I took the excuse to go down south for a little bit. Get some sun and get away from Springfield. After bumming around D.C. for a while, I went to the beach. That was where I met Carlos working on a fishing boat in North Carolina. By the time I got clean, got my heart broken and came limping back, they had become a family.

I remember the picnic we had in Forest Park after they picked me up from the bus station. Edgar was so excited to see me he kept waving the cheap blue plastic fish I brought him like it was a trophy. Kianna was doing the Frankenstein walk with her arms outstretched, throwing her weight from one foot to the other, while Callie would wait on her knees with her arms open to catch her. Juan, I remember, was quiet that day, but nice enough, carrying the paper sack of food and giving Edgar a shoulder ride when he begged. The thing I remember most about the day though is the way Edgar and Kianna seemed so like brother and sister. Edgar would walk slowly backwards holding her hands for support so she could stumble forwards. Whenever he would go off to play on the swings, she would cry and try to follow until he gave up the swings and came back to her. It was obvious that he was her whole universe and in many ways she was his. This gave me a good feeling and I was just at the beginning of having any feelings at all after such a long time of being high all the time that I actually had to look away from them a few times so I wouldn't embarrass myself by crying. It was Carlos who taught me how to feel, who showed me that all that drugging was covering over my feelings and that feelings were not a bad thing to have. Of course then he broke my heart and then feelings were suddenly a terrible thing to have. Luckily I toughed it out and didn't fall back into all that. Instead I decided to go back to school, and get on with my life. Sometimes I think I chose accounting because I wanted to be able to account for things, or get back some order I had lost.

When I was a boy, order was important to me, to the disapproval of my overbearing father who felt that was a sissy trait. I liked to have my toys lined up, my closet organized, my books from tallest to shortest. Then I felt in control of things. That all seems so long ago and yet it has come around full circle—the self coming home to the self.

"Where will we be going to school?" Kianna's voice sounds little. I bet all this time she was thinking about Ms. Faith and her peer meditation group.

"Does Ms. Jones really run a peer meditation group?"

Kianna laughs. "*Mediation*. Not meditation. It's peer mediation. You know, kids helping each other work out problems? Ever heard of it?"

"Not really."

"Not really?"

"Well, I've heard of the words, but I've never heard anything about the things Ms. Jones does."

"You can't do it until fifth grade and even then you have to write a essay and get a teacher to write you a letter saying you'd be good and you have to show you're good at getting all your work done."

"Were you planning on doing it?"

She is quiet for a minute, and I can't tell what she is thinking about, what's the holdup.

"Were you?" I ask again.

"Yeah," she says, and that's it. Subject closed.

I feel bad about being angry with her before and telling her to sit back. It's got to be pretty lonely back there all by herself. "Do you want to sit up front for a while?" I ask her.

"Really?"

I look along the side of the highway for a place to stop and let her come up front, but there's not much of a shoulder in this stretch. I debate the safety issues and decide to throw caution into the wind. "Sure, climb over the seat and sit up here for a bit." I move the map off the seat and try to slide it onto the dashboard but it's too narrow.

Kianna comes over one leg at a time until her curly head of hair is right there next to me. "Buckle up," I say in greeting, handing her the map.

She rifles around looking for both ends of the seat belt, disturbing Edgar from his trance.

"Cut it out," he grumbles, pulling off his head-phones.

"Move over, I can't get the buckle," she says.

"Get back there, you're all on me." He pushes her with his elbow.

"Ow, cut it!" she yells at him.

"Okay you two, enough. Edgar push over and make room for your sister or take the back." I honestly don't know which he'll do, but he pushes over and Kianna finds the buckle and clicks the belt into it. She looks up, happy and satisfied. She surveys the road ahead and then the items I've handed her.

"Can I put on the radio?" she asks.

"Sure," I answer, letting my elbow jut out the window.

"Only FM," commands Edgar, fingering his chains the way he does.

Kianna fiddles with the old push buttons, getting mostly static, one classical station, and then she hits a song she knows and stops. Edgar groans, but he doesn't make her change it.

The sky has that end-of-the-day feeling to it as we ride along three in a row in my new car towards Florida. One song becomes the next, and my mind is wandering until I suddenly realize that we are all three singing along to the same song. "Riding that train..." we sing together, getting louder with each refrain until we are all aware that we are doing it, singing out loud, together.

In this moment I feel truly happy.

Chapter 6
Connecticut

He asks me if I have a book and I want to strangle him. I know I have *anger management issues.* I can hear Miss J's voice in my head, see her black face as she tilts her head to get my eyes, make me smile. It always worked too. My fists would unclench themselves and I would be able to breathe again. Something about the way she said *anger management issues* made me know she was making fun of it even while she was telling me the truth.

The first time she said it was after she caught me busting on the school wall so that, in the end, my hand was fat and bloody. Nobody could get me to stop so they called Miss J. She didn't yell or nothing. She didn't even order me to stop. I remember real clear how she just leaned up against the wall I was punching and looked in my face. Then slowly she reached up and touched my hand. She wasn't forcing it not to hit again or nothing, she was just resting her hand there. I remember then I had to work real hard not to cry. Something about her hand on my hand made me want to bawl.

I could hear whitey calling everyone back into class, "Okay everybody, it's all over now, come back into class."

We stood that way in the hall for a while until I could get a hold of myself and then, like she knew, Miss J said, "Come on, let's take a walk," and off she walks like she knows I'm going to follow her, and I do. I know we're going up to the Planning Center.

That was the day she said about the anger thing and at first I was shaking my head like she was crazy because I really thought it was wacked, but the more stuff she said and the more times I went up there, the more it started making sense. Though I still don't get what she means when she says it's in my control because it's so not in my control.

Kianna had a fit in the rest stop and she's was hiding in the bathroom, but she then she came out. Finally.

She is messed up, that kid, jumping me in public like that. The thing is no matter how pissed I get I can't help worrying about her. It's another thing that's not in my control. I try to walk away and say forget it, she's not my problem, but before long I can't stop thinking she's hurt or lost or something. She has always needed so much looking after; always thinking she can do anything and nearly getting killed over and over. Like the time she went out on the roof to get the hurt pigeon, just went out the open window onto the roof like she wasn't three stories off the ground. Talking about some research project. I had to go haul her in before someone called DSS again, and she's kicking and hollering like I was hurting her. It was bad.

What I'm trying to figure now is how to get outa this whole scene. I seen Luis's stupid MapQuest sitting on the seat, and I'm trying to pick where to take off.

I'm thinking maybe New York because I hear it's a big city and I could mix it in there. Also, it's a big place so I can find a new posse without too much trouble, maybe run some errands or drugs if I have to until I get set up there.

"What do you think Ms. Faith Jones is doing just now?" This comes from Luis. What is he asking about Miss J for? Does he even know her?

"Ms. Faith Jones. What do you think she's doing right now?" he asks again.

"Um, maybe she's leading peer mediation," Kianna says.

"That's Mondays," I can't help myself.

"What day is it?" she asks.

"Tuesday," Luis answers.

"Middle school," I say at the same time as Kianna.

Then the two a them get into a whole thing about what she does in Middle School, rifting on violence prevention and they got it all wrong. I shake my head at them.

"So then what does she do with the middle school?" Luis presses.

"Talks," I tell them.

"Talks?" He is so stupid.

Kianna is so nosey wanting to know what the talk's about.

"Stuff." I say to get her off my back.

"What kinda stuff?" she presses.

"Stuff about how to fix your problems." I don't want to tell them. I feel my fist clench and I know now this means I am getting angry. Why does this make me angry?

The trees whiz by. I squint my eyes until they are a blur of color. Because it is my business, that's why. They need to step back from my business.

"How to solve them peacefully right?" Kianna's still at it like a dog with a bone.

"Right."

"That's violence prevention stupid." My fists dig into the seat on each side.

I make my mind go blank. I do that thing Miss J told me about, that works if I want it to, where I picture nothing, just like a blank piece of paper, no lines or holes or writing, just white. I picture it real hard until my fists unclench. Then I slide my headphones on and I go into the music. I leave the anger and go off with the music, just leave with it.

I am leaving. That's the truth. I have never been outa Springfield before and I am on the road, leaving it, driving away to start over again. Goodbye school, goodbye punks on Union Street, goodbye boys I owe money to, goodbye Sonia and your sweet lips. Sonia. I feel in my pocket for the charm she gave me off her bracelet. It's still there, but I don't take it out, just finger it. I pull the picture of her down from the sky, her long black braids, the shadow of her lashes, her shape in my arms. I am thinking like a girl now, thinking like that, but I can't help the way she makes me feel and anyway no one is reading my mind.

I look over my shoulder to see if Kianna is reading my mind, but she stares out the window, her face all sad.

Like the last time DSS split us up when Momi went missing after Juan got locked up. I remember that day, Kianna sitting frozen on our ragged couch with that same sad look on her face while the lousy social worker tells us there's no foster place for us together, but we'll both still be in the same school, and anyway it's temporary. Boxhead.

My fist's clenched in my lap while she's saying all this, talking real slow like we don't understand English, and I see her looking over all nervous thinking I'm going to blow up and hurt her or something. Then I think I might. I picture bashing her head into the mirror on the wall behind her and watching her crack in a million pieces. But then somehow Kianna knows this and she says, "Don't do nothing Edgar." Which only makes the social worker more nervous and she takes out her cell phone and calls her office.

I hated that crap foster home. It was three weeks and I thought about taking off every day, except I kinda wanted to see if Kianna was making it to school, so I'd go and then by the time I was there things seemed normal again and around lunchtime Miss J would come by real casual like she wasn't checking up on me or nothing, but I knew she was. I didn't care though. A couple times when I lost my mind over nothing, I would go up to the Planning Center and play chess. She has a board up there and she taught me what all the pieces do and it wasn't too hard to remember after the first couple times. I told her everything that was happening because what do I care that Juan's in jail. He's not my father. Miss J asked all questions about how long he's been living with us and I admit it's a pretty long time since I was four, ten years, but still, he don't mean nothing to me. The part that burns is that Momi took off on us. I didn't see that coming.

The school called Luis over that, but he didn't do nothing I could tell. Alright once he took me and Kianna out on a weekend to get outa those crappy houses, but that's all. Kianna said hers wasn't so bad, but she could a been lying so I wouldn't get mad. I seen how her hair wasn't done for days and her clothes looked all messed up. Momi would have had a fit to see her looking like that in school. But then it was her fault Kianna was looking like that.

Momi messed up bad that time. I didn't talk to her when the social worker came to get me out from there and took me back to that ugly office to see Momi. She was all up in my grill, happy to see me and hugging on me, and I just went dead and looked the other way. When they brought Kianna I could see she didn't know what to do neither. With all them workers were watching us, we had to act like it's okay or maybe they wouldn't give her back the custody. Still I didn't say anything to her for a long time after what she done.

Maybe that's why she went and killed herself like that. I don't know.

Kianna climbs over the seat pushing into me. I tell her to quit it but Luis's making her wear the stupid seat belt so she's digging around for it under me.

I tell her again to cut it and she starts mouthing.

"Okay you two, enough. Edgar push over and make room for your sister or take the back."

I think about stretching out on the back seat, but he'll probably make me wear the seat belt too, so I just hold my seat.

Then she puts on the crappy radio a his.

She pushes buttons and stops on the cool stuff. She has good taste in music—I didn't see that coming.

Then she lands a good one. The windows are down and the air starting to cool off. If it was still boiling hot, I'd have to take the back, but for now the tunes are good and the road is looking smooth. Driving that train, high on cocaine.

I wonder if Luis has ever done cocaine, or any drug in his whole sorry life. He is such a pleaser the way he is always following all the rules. I can't stand that. He had on that self-help tape earlier and it was just begging me to throw it out the window. All that relax your stupid mind and body. What is the point of that? I got something in my jacket could relax his mind and body.

That's what I shoulda done at the last rest stop, instead of eating a soggy burrito. Made my stomach feel bad and killed my high from before.

"Can we stop anytime soon?" I ask like I don't really care.

"We'll cross state lines in the next ten miles or so. Can you hold out until then?" Luis asks.

I nod.

"I thought maybe we'd combine it with a stop for dinner. Find a real restaurant, not just a rest stop place. What do you think?" he asks.

I think all that singing has put Luis in a good mood. I nod again and reach over to flip the station.

"Hey," Kianna says like she doesn't want to give it up.

"Hey," I imitate her like she hates.

"Edgar," she says annoyed.

"Edgar," I say annoyed.

"Cut it out!" She's getting mad.

I love this. "Cut it out!" I copy her voice.

"I mean it," she threatens.

"I mean it." I want to howl over the twisted up look on her face, but then I think I catch a note of the Beastie Boys and I flip back and forth to try and find it. "Shit," I accidentally say out loud when I can't get it.

"Watch your mouth!" she practically yells at me and I know she is thinking of the last rest stop. My palm itches with the thought of it.

"Sorry," I say, meaning for slapping her, but maybe she thinks I mean for saying it.

She doesn't say nothing after that so I can't tell, but I let her take over the flipping until she comes up with a weather report. She stops at it and we all listen.

"Well, folks, if April showers were supposed to bring May flowers they haven't yet, because we are in for more showers. Partly cloudy tonight with lows in the upper fifties, chance of thundershowers later tonight, then warmer tomorrow with light rain in the morning, turning heavier in the afternoon." Great, a wet car trip.

"Then I say let's do more driving tonight, so we can stop early tomorrow night. What do you say we try to make New Jersey before we turn in?" says Luis.

This all means nothing to me and I try to picture a map. I should have paid closer attention in school. Is that before New York? I want to ask, but I don't want to look stupid again so I keep it shut.

"Aw," Kianna says, "I wanted to see New York City." And I love her for saying that and for knowing where the states are.

"Well, the city is expensive. Even parking is a lot of money. We'd be better to just go by it altogether." Uncle Luis, the maseta.

"It'd be a cultural experience," Kianna tries.

But Luis ain't going for it.

"Maybe another time." He's got to realize that he is dumping us in Miami, that there won't be another time. But he leans over and turns up the music.

I understand why he's dumping us; that he wants us out of Springfield before they make a stink that Kianna has a different mother. Luis already told me this back when I was refusing to pack up. But when I told him I don't understand why he couldn't come up with a better relative than his old mother, he said it ain't up to him, that's who the court gave us to. He acted like it was a good thing they decided we got to go together, but I'm still stuck on the got to go part.

Only one time in my whole life did Abuela come to meet me and that was before Kianna came. I was pretty young so I can't say as I remember everything about it. What I do remember is her phony "Kootchy Coo" routine with me and the way she spoke like razors to Momi. I would hide behind Momi's legs from Abuela and this made Abuela so mad she threw a pot of coffee that splashed when it hit the floor and since I was the closest thing to the ground, it got on me and burnt my feet.

That was the end of her visit. It was also the first time DSS came snooping around. Some ER doctor must have reported that Momi was lying when she said I spilled it on myself. She always was a terrible liar. They didn't take me away that time, just came to the old apartment on Union, the one we was in before Juan and Kianna came.

I liked that apartment. It was cool the way we were on the top floor and could see the lit-up basketball from the Basketball Hall of Fame. It took until we moved for me to know that wasn't the moon; my own personal big orange moon right out my window. Every night, no matter what else was going down, there was my moon. Those days Momi worked nights and Maria was in charge of me. She'd give me my bath and put me in my little bed on the floor next to Momi's bed and I'd lie there staring at my orange moon until I couldn't keep my eyes open anymore. When I'd open them there would be Momi, smiling down at me with her finger to her lips to be quiet, it was still early. Then we'd get into the big bed and she'd fall asleep right away. Sometimes I would go back to sleep too, but sometimes I just lay there, watching the shadows as light came into the room from morning.

I think it was those days with the orange moon that first got me interested in stars. I remember all the time wondering what a star was and then, when I was five, I first went to the planetarium at the science museum. When I found out it was a big ball of gases, my head was spinning that something could be so different than it looked. I wanted to know more. I wanted to go back there every day, only it was like a year before we went again. By then I started collecting old books out from the giveaway boxes on anything to do with space. Only I couldn't read them. Every time Luis came over, I'd get him to read me one since he could read, but then when I found out he was light, I didn't want to sit on the couch with him no more.

By that time though, I already learned about galaxies. It takes a big mind to imagine a billion galaxies. That's what they say coasts in the cosmos, a billion systems of stars. A billion. I keep trying to picture a billion of anything but I can't get out of hundreds of thousands even. It's just way too many. When I get done in, I think about something specific, like the moon. Now the moon is cool because even though it's shaped like the basketball over the Hall of Fame, it has these actual phases, and the phases have these wacked names I like to think in my head sometimes, like crescent and gibbous and second quarter, which if you think about it in math two quarters is half, so it's really a fancy way to say half moon. These are calming words to me though and I repeat one or the other of them in my head for different effect. Take crescent, that's a pointy word, shaped like a curved knife blade. I use that one when I'm mad about something or like when I want revenge, I say *crescent crescent crescent* over in my head until it passes. Second quarter is like a trickster word, so I think that one when I'm lying so my face won't show the lie, or even when I'm just hiding something, I repeat it in my head. Gibbous is my most special. It's for the lopsided phase when the moon is getting bigger or smaller and it's that in-between phase. I say this one when I need love or safety. That sounds wacked, but it's the truth. I think it started because it sounds kinda like *give us*. The first time I used it was when me and Kianna was going to be taken when a neighbor called the police on Momi and Popi for screaming. It worked too, they didn't take us that time.

I used it another time when I was first hooking up with Sonia and we were in the hall alone on accident, just standing there side by side and my hands started sweating. It just came into my head without me planning it, *gibbous gibbous gibbous*. And then I got real calm, and I just looked right into her face. Her hair was in those tight braids and her skin looked real smooth so close up, smooth and chocolaty. Then her real long black lashes fluttered and she looked right at me. I could feel her curves and see the tops of her breasts even without looking down. We just stared on each other until whitey poked her big nose out and told us to *rejoin the class now*. But anyway it was already sealed. She was my girl.

"Get those papers off the floor, will you Edgar?" Luis needs the directions.

I reach down, pull them up and I'm about to hand them over.

"What does it say to do on there?" He wants me to read them. I look at all the words and they start their swimming around the page. "Does it say the Tappan Zee or the George Washington Bridge?" I scan for the word bridge, which I know starts with a *b*, but these damn directions have so many words on them. I found *B-R*, but that's the closest thing and that looks too short to say a word like bridge.

Kianna leans into me looking at the paper and in a minute answers, "George Washington."

I look up at her.

"Right here," she points for me, like I'm stupid. I'm not stupid.

"That doesn't say bridge," I say.

"B-R stands for bridge." She doesn't say it meanly but I feel mad anyway. I push the papers at her and reach for my headphones. They've fallen to the floor too and I push off to reach them all strapped up in this seatbelt like a straightjacket.

"Ow! That hurts," she cries like a big baby.

"Shut up," which is what I wanted to say before.

"That's enough now," Luis says. "Did you say George Washington? There are so many signs now, I'm getting confused."

"Yes," Kianna answers him. "What's that light?" She points to the dashboard.

"I don't know," he answers.

"The gas," I say.

"We're out of gas!" Luis sounds like he's going all-out panic now.

"Easy," I say.

"We can just get off at the next exit." Kianna sounds like when she's talking Momi into something she said no to. I look real hard at the sign coming up and even though it's moving I can make out the word *New*. Then I get it. We are going to get off for gas in New York City.

Uncle Luis is fretting. He can be such a boxhead.

"This is the last exit before the bridge," Kianna tells him. He puts on his blinker to get off.

When he does there is no gas station in sight.

"Take a left," Kianna tells him, like she's been here before, like she knows.

He does it. I look over and see his thin lips pressed tight together.

Streetlights are coming on and it looks like home. I can picture my boys over on the other corner, Brock, Fifty and Killer Cam leaning on the side of a building. I want to get out and walk over there to them, offer them my paw in the handshake of The Bloods.

Next corner comes by, I see a couple of geeked-out crackheads there. One of them has got so many spots on his face they look like craters on the moon.

"It says we're in Harlem now," Kianna reports. How does she know how to read all them words she's never seen before?

She always was the best reader, figuring stuff off my books before I ever could. When Momi still had a job, we'd sit at the table before school and she'd read the cereal boxes, when she was in kindergarten! It's so obvious we're not related. I was glad when we started having breakfast at school, so I could eat with my friends and get away from hearing all the ingredients. I only want to know so much.

"This isn't good." Luis's worrying.

Luis never owned a car before. He probably thinks as soon as that light goes on we're done for. I know better though. Jaquan's brother Kevin had this broken down piece a junk and no money for gas, and we'd ride for days over to Eastern Avenue and back on red. Then he started dealing and soon he be flossing, wearing his new sneakers and gold chains. Then he never took me and Jaquan with him no more.

Luis is sweating for the first time all day and it's just now finally cooling off. I see Kianna is catching his bug too, squirming and getting all fussed.

"Take it easy," I say to the two of them. "We got plenty to get us there. Chill. Enjoy the sights." I point to a lit up bar with a crescent moon in blue lights. I think this is a good sign.

"There!" Kianna yells, pointing her finger. A few blocks down there looks to be a gas station.

"Well done," Luis says, wiping his forehead with the back of his hand.

But when we get up there we see that the pump handles are missing and the front window has big strips a tape holding the broken pane together.

Luis puts the car in park. We all stare in the broken window at the burnt-out station.

"Shit," Kianna says, and somehow this time when she says it, it's funny. I snort and before you know it we are all laughing.

A bum wanders up in messed up clothes and Uncle Luis calls to him.

"Hey, where's the nearest gas station?"

"*Que?*" the bum asks and Kianna asks him again in Spanish. The man scratches his dirty whiskers and then gives a bunch of directions. After that he holds out his hand. Luis fishes in his pocket and gives the guy a few bucks and then pulls out.

"See, I told you New York was expensive. You even have to pay for directions." He says this to be funny and now we are all in a good mood. It's strange how some-thing like the right word, at the right time, can make everything seem all right. Or maybe it's how she said it. Or maybe it's just that we have her here between us.

Chapter 7
New York

If Uncle Luis doesn't say something to me soon I might have to hit him on the back of his square head and make his glasses pop off the front. What did he think I was doing in the rest stop bathroom, my nails? Doesn't he care about me at all? All he'd have to say is something like "Are you okay?" and that would be enough for me. Or even if he put on that dumb tape again, but he just sits there staring straight ahead and it's so quiet in here I could scream.

Imagine if I suddenly just started to scream and wouldn't stop. Edgar would get all mad and try to hit me to make me shut up, and Uncle Luis would be swerving all over the road like my voice was a bunch of darts hitting him. Is it wrong that that makes me smile? The idea that I could make them both crazy so easy?

It's them or me at this point. Really I could go crazy back here with nothing to do and no one to talk to. Studies show things die of neglect. I read that in last months' *Time for Kids*. Sure, they meant plants but it probably stretches to all living things and I am a goddamn living thing. Swearing makes me feel better sometimes.

Sometimes it doesn't. Like back there when I said shit out loud and Edgar slapped me. I know better than that. I know he just doesn't want me to have a street mouth, that he wants me to grow up right and he thinks he's the only one I got left to keep me straight. I know. Sometimes though the devil gets into me. That's what Father Brown says anyway. Edgar doesn't know about Father Brown because I've been sneaking to church. Mrs. Perez took me there the first time once when I was locked out the apartment and sitting in the hall where she kept tripping over me. I don't want to make a big deal out of it, but all that chanting makes me feel better. And the candles. Mrs. Perez introduced me to Father Brown over there and now I go see him whenever I want. He calls them "our little chats" and that makes me smile. They're kinda like my chats with Miss Faith, only different.

I've had a lot of time on my hands lately. I think that's why I keep going down to that church. Well, that and because they had that big book drive. I got tons of books for me and a few real nice astronomy books for Edgar. He doesn't let on that he likes them, but I seen he packed two of them and another couple he had under his bed. I don't know why he likes hard books he can't read, but maybe it's that the pictures are real nice. Sometimes I want to just read them out loud to him, but I already learned the hard way not to read to him. Maybe he'll learn to read in Miami.

"Where will we be going to school?" It just popped out of my mouth when I swore it was going to be Uncle

Luis who spoke the first word. Especially after he got me into it with Edgar and made the car go all quiet.

"Does Ms. Faith Jones really run a peer meditation group?" He's still thinking about that. I can't help but laugh at his mistake.

I correct him and he takes it pretty well and even admits he's never heard of it. Or at least he's never heard about Miss Faith doing it. It's funny how he always says her whole name, like he's not sure it's okay to call her by just her first name. The teachers at my school are all different and like to be called different ways. It's real different than the other schools in the city, but I've been there so long, it's not strange to me.

Uncle Luis asks me more about it and then he puts up a sore question about me joining. I really wanted to do it, and every year I was bothering Miss Faith to let me in early, but she said every time that I had to wait until fifth grade.

"Well, were you?" Uncle Luis asks me again.

His question reminds me that we are driving to Miami, that I don't live in Springfield anymore, that Momi is dead. My stomach hurts.

"Yeah," I say, and that's it. I am ready to fall into the bad feeling he just opened up, but then he surprises me and asks me if I want to come up front. This is just what I need: a change of scenery.

I climb over and turn on the radio. It is still hot and I feel sticky sitting between Edgar and Uncle Luis, especially without that sweater for under my legs, but at the same time it is comforting after being back there all alone for so long. I can actually tell where I begin and end, so I don't mind the heat anymore.

Music is so great. I love it. The way it lifts you up inside and brings you all these places. I am searching around for the songs that make me go somewhere.

There's one about wheels on a gravel road and I kinda want to stop there, but Edgar hates anything country. One about wanting to fly, nope. Then I come on the one about not breathing whenever I think about you. I leave it here for a minute, just long enough to close my eyes and imagine what she might be talking about. I can feel it in the way she is singing, but I can't really understand it. It's like square root. I can almost get the picture of that, the root of the square, but then just before I have it, it disappears on me and I am back to straight calculations. Edgar's real good a picturing stuff but not as much at explaining what he sees. So I tried asking Popi about it once, just before he went to jail, but he seemed all mad that I was learning something so stupid. He just muttered in Spanish about what are they teaching me down at that Montessori school.

The funny thing about remembering that is, I remember he said it in Spanish. I used to not notice when things were in Spanish and when they were in English and the back and forth seemed natural, but lately I've noticed I am more and more in English, thinking it, talking it and dreaming it. Maybe I'm becoming English and soon I'll say things like *pip pip cheerio* and *all right then*. Maybe if I start doing that when we get to Miami, my grandmother will have to send me back to Springfield. She'll wipe her hands on her apron and toss them up in the air in disgust and say, "*Mi Dios, qué pasa?*"

I can't really picture my grandmother, though Edgar says she's ugly and he'd rather hang than live with her. I wonder why he is coming along at all, why he hasn't run off yet, gone to Brock or Fifty or one of the other boys from the street. It would be easy to get lost in Springfield long enough for Uncle Luis to have given up and just left with me.

I figure he's up to something. He probably has some big plan to get lost in New York, knowing Edgar. Maybe he has a phone number rolled up in his pocket of some dealer to call to set him up and he's figuring it'd be safer to surf a new city then have to look over his back for DSS and KEY and all the other grown-ups in Springfield who don't let Edgar's stern face and beginning whiskers fool them.

I remember a few months ago when I had to go real bad and I busted in on him in the bathroom shaving his face with Momi's pink BIC razor. I laughed so hard I peed my pants and I hadn't done that in a real long time. It was funny to find him like that, half lathered up and half shaved peering into the mirror like his eyes were going bad, but it was even funnier to see him see me, his eyes all bugging out and his skin flushing red. I thought that was the best until I saw what he did next.

After that day, he started sliding the lock on the door and so I had to be real sneaky to see what he was doing in there. But this one day, I was up early and I decided to do like a stake out. I took my blanket into the nasty tub and pulled the grimy curtain closed around it. Then I sat down in there and waited. It took a long time for Edgar to come in and I was counting cracked tiles and figuring out square roots when he finally did. I sat real still so as not to give myself up. He did his business and then I heard the toilet flush and the water go on. I heard the water splashing like he's washing his face and then it went quiet out there. I hadn't planned it too well because now how was I going to see what he was up to without pulling back the curtain and getting a smack from him. I really wanted to know though so I looked around and sure enough there's a cut in the plastic curtain. Real slow and careful I poked it bigger and looked through there. What I saw him doing shocked me to silence, which was good because if I'd found it funny I'd have been done for. There at the mirror was Edgar with Momi's tweezers pulling out his eyebrow hairs one at a time, all the ones growing in between anyway. I couldn't believe my brother was doing all that stuff in the bathroom about his hair, and then I realized what was going on and it all made sense: Edgar had got a girl.

It hit me square between the eyes and I felt the shock of it fill the tub around me. My brother had a girlfriend and he was trying to make himself all perfect for her.

I waited a long time in that tub, so long that the cold came up through my blanket, until Edgar left and I could climb out all stiff legged. I decided then and there that I was going to figure out which girl right off.

It wasn't even hard really. Going to the same school has its up sides. By the end of the day I knew she was black and her name was Sonia. She has a sister in the class across the hall and a brother in one of the classes downstairs.

After that I started watching for her and seeing how she acts. She comes for her sister every day after the bell rings and I have to admit she's pretty nice to her, standing there waiting even when her sister is taking forever to get ready. I've also seen her downstairs at her brother's class in the morning sometimes when me and Edgar come in late and we have to get a pass from the office. This one morning a few weeks ago her brother was bawling and she was kneeling down and hugging him real nice. That was the day I decided it was all right with me if she wanted to be Edgar's girl. I never said anything to him because I wasn't supposed to even know about her, but I'd have to be real stupid not to see how they look at each other. Even the day her brother was bawling, she still noticed Edgar coming into school. She looked up and gave him a half smile and he dipped his head at her. That was all, but I saw it. I know what I saw.

After that I started noticing how pretty she was, how her hair was always done up real careful and her eyes looked so kind. She smiled at me once. I don't know if she knew I'm Edgar's sister or if she's just that nice to everybody, but I liked it.

Love Will Keep Us Together, that is so not true, I hate that song. It makes my stomach hurt worse. I quick flip right off to a new station. Then I find a keeper, one we can sing along with. It has cocaine in it, which is a drug I know, but the tune is so killer that I can't resist it. Before too long, just as I knew, we're all singing with it.

Uncle Luis is funny when he sings. He opens his mouth like he's in chorus or something. He makes his lips do the exact letters instead of like Edgar who sings barely moving his mouth at all. I look from one to the other seeing how different they are from each other. Uncle Luis is light-skinned and everything about him is small. His nose is small, his glasses are small, and his lips, and his shoulders. His body is like one skinny man and I wonder if he has that AIDS. Maybe that's why he's getting rid of us like this. Maybe he is sick and dying and he wants to save us the grief of losing him too.

I look closer at him. His face is all lit up and happy while he's singing and I think, "Nah, he can't be dying. He wouldn't be this happy if he was dying." But then I think Momi was his sister and she just died, how could he be happy? I haven't felt happy since then. Not even once.

My stomach's feeling weird. Not like hungry exactly but like a tightness, like a snake is gripping me in there. Is that the feeling of losing Momi? Will I have it forever now?

I look over at Edgar. I see a few stray hairs growing in on the underside of his left eyebrow, but other than that his dark eyebrows are beautifully shaped. Edgar is an artist making his face look like that. His lip has a little stubble on it and he has a couple pimples here and there, but his hair is gelled down on his head perfectly. He also has some bad dark circles under his eyes that weren't there the last time I looked at him real close.

Which was when? When was the last time I looked real close up at Edgar's face? I can't even think of it now, and it is something I used to do regularly. I think I know Edgar's face about as good as I know anything in this world. I for sure looked at it more than my own face, which is scrawny and has nothing particularly fine about it. My friend Tenise says she thinks my face has real prudential which I thought was something about insurance, but she seemed to say it like it was something better than that.

I keep looking all the time for signs of Momi in my face. Just one thing of her beauty to come up in my face would be enough, but so far nothing's come. Every day I picture her face in my mind to be sure I won't forget it before I have something that looks like her to look at. I guess for now I got Edgar because he sure looks a whole lot like her, especially since he made his eyebrows shaped better. It would be a real shame if Edgar turned out more beautiful than me.

I reach up and tilt the rearview mirror down to look at myself. Maybe something new showed up over all those hours in the back seat. Uncle Luis doesn't say anything so I twist it so I can see myself. Nah, same me as when we left Pine Street. Same dull frizzy black hair. Same nothing face. Same front teeth came in crooked. Tenise says they're not, but I know she's talking junk when she says that. We were learning a geometry lesson on lines and I swear Ms. L almost used my teeth as an example of divergent, but then she looked past me and pointed to the hands on the clock instead. Whatever. That's what Stacey says all the time about everything. Whatever.

I look over at Edgar to see if I look anything like him. He's all crumpled now, but usually looks real nice with his black hair cut short close to his head and his dark eyebrows curved nice around his black eyes with real long eyelashes like stripes off his lids. I look back in the mirror at my eyelashes and see they are short, stumpy nothing lashes. I push the mirror away—that's enough a that.

I look the other way at Luis and see we be sitting in light-to-dark order. His hair and skin are lighter than mine and I be lighter than Edgar who's got all the looks in this car if you ask me. Uncle Luis has a funny small nose, like a white person nose and his glasses are perched there like a scared bird. His brown hair is curling at his ears and he doesn't have any on his face. I look real close to see whiskers but even though it's afternoon I don't see much there.

Edgar asks if we can stop and I imagine us in New York City with all the shining lights and colorful billboards. Uncle Luis is so cheap though, he says no, we're going around the city. I really want to see what it's like. I want to see Broadway and all those famous people coming and going, the streets just filled with them.

One time Ramona went to the city and she came back with these real tall boots that zipped up the back and she was walking all in a strut like she got something no one else on earth was ever going to get. Not that the boots were so great, she had to sit out at gym and she couldn't do a thing at the park, but just that she had something so different, from the city. She said it was her Mama that bought them for her, but I heard it was her next-door neighbor that took pity on her because her mother drinks too much. Either way, those boots made me want to see the city for myself, more than just on a postcard that Xoshell sent around at sharing in Miss Munoz's class. She had this collection from when her father lived there and he'd send her different ones now and then. She acted like she didn't want anyone to read the back, but really I think that's why she brought them in in the first place, so we'd all read the back and see somebody loved her, she wasn't going to be living with her grandmother forever. Me, I liked the one of that big fancy hotel at night with all the lights lit up so bright. The Plaza, was what it was called, the Plaza Hotel. Xoshell was going on about how her father lived there, but even in lower elementary we all knew she was just blowing smoke with that one.

I wasn't going to say anything to her about it because that was right around when Popi had to go away and I didn't want any of the kids making a big deal about it. I even got kinda mad when Miss Faith brought it up, like it was perfectly normal. She did it in private and everything, but still it made me feel annoyed that she would just out and talk about it.

I remember it was just the beginning of spring and she had the window of her office open for the first time and she was making a big deal out of it. Miss Faith is kinda a nature freak, plus she gets real excited about the weirdest stuff. Anyway she was making a big deal of smelling the air like it was perfume.

"Smell that air Kianna?" she asked me.

"No." I wasn't going in on it. "I don't smell nothin."

"Nothing? Go on, take a big sniff," she tells me.

I must have looked at her funny because she was asking me what, like she didn't know all that sniffing is strange.

"Really, you can smell spring coming. If you close your eyes and let the smell come into you, spring happens in your mind. Try it."

Sometimes I can't help myself and even if I don't want to I get caught up in what Miss Faith is going on about.

"Come on, I'll close the office door so no one sees and we'll just try it for a minute." And sure enough she closed her door and came back over, sat down and closed her eyes. I felt stupid about doing it, but curious too, so I closed my eyes for just a minute. I wasn't going to take a big smell like she said, but I did listen with my nose and it was a big surprise what happened next. I saw flowers, like the ones that grow at the park, those bright red and yellow ones. My eyes popped open in surprise that she was right and I just sat there saying nothing until she opened her eyes up.

One thing I like about Miss Faith is that she doesn't make you do anything and she doesn't rub it in when she is right, which is good because she turns out to be right a lot of the time. When she opened her eyes, she didn't ask about the flowers but what she said surprised me just as much.

"So how do you feel about your dad going to jail?"

Just like that. She said it just like that, like it was something normal to talk about. Now I know a lot of kids whose parents have gone to jail, it's not that, it's just that it's not something you talk about out in the open like she was.

I didn't know what to say, and when I don't know what to say, I get mad. It's just something that has always happened and sometimes now I see it coming so I don't have to act mad even when I feel mad, like in lessons with Ms. L when she asks me something and I don't know the answer I feel mad for a second, but now I don't act mad I just shrug and she doesn't make a big deal of me not knowing and the feeling goes away. But that day, I got real toasty mad at Miss Faith when she asked me that. I wanted to be out of there so bad that I nearly jumped up and just left, but when I looked over at her and she was smiling, I just couldn't do it to her.

"Nothin'," I tried, shrugging.

"Hmmm," she said kinda quiet.

"What you mean by that?" I asked in my picking-a-fight voice.

She looked at me long and hard because we've been friends a long time and she knows all my tricks. I wanted to have a tantrum then, to just let loose the way I used to when I first started going to Miss Faith after I threw that chair in kindergarten.

"Get those papers off the floor, will you Edgar?" Uncle Luis needs his MapQuest directions.

"What does it say to do on there?" He wants Edgar to read them. An anxious feeling starts in my stomach over this. He asks which bridge we should be taking.

I know plain Edgar can't read anything on there and I wait a minute until I can get my normal voice and then I blurt out "George Washington!" like I'm just too excited to wait.

Edgar looks at me.

"Right here." I point for him to see the words I read.

"That doesn't say bridge," he says.

I don't understand what makes something so easy for me so hard for Edgar but I say real quiet so Uncle Luis won't hear. "*B-R* stands for bridge."

At that he pushes the papers at me giving up like he always does and reaching for his stupid headphones pushing me to get them.

That's when we figure out we're running outa gas. Uncle Luis gets all hands flappy and Edgar has to cool him down.

Then I see we are in New York City!

When I suggest we get off Uncle Luis does it! He gets off in New York City!

When he does though, there is no gas station in sight. He doesn't know what to do and I don't want him getting right back on the highway so I start directing him. He does what I tell him and before you know it, it looks like we're driving up Eastern Avenue with all the crackheads and the bums. I see a sign ahead that says we're in Harlem.

I've got to pee and I have a funny feeling, but I am distracted by the neighborhood and the people. Uncle Luis finds a station, but it's all wrecked and abandoned.

"Shit," I say without thinking. But instead of flying off the handle this time Edgar just laughs. I can't figure him.

The sky is losing light now and lights are coming on. Uncle Luis asks a bum where there's another gas station and we follow along the way the guy said. It's taking a long time, but finally we find it and I get out and am running to the bathroom right as soon as Uncle Luis gets out. The door is locked and I have to go into the greasy station for the key. My underwear feels a little wet down there when I'm walking but I think maybe it is from being so hot all day. I prolly shouldn't a been sitting on the fancy sweater.

Now it is dark and the lights are on inside and the man there is big and tall with a flat head and the biggest muscles on his arms, like it's a Halloween costume.

"Can I have the bathroom key?" I try to sound normal.

He doesn't say anything, just points to a long piece of wood with a key strapped on the end with a piece of wire.

"Thanks."

I go back out into the night, which seems even darker now, and around the side of the station to the locked door. The key doesn't go right in because the lock is messed up, like someone stuck a fork in there and bent it, or a knife, but I finally get it in and push the heavy door open.

The smell is worse than I was ready for and I switch to breathing through my mouth right away. I feel on the wall for the light switch and when I turn it on I almost wish I hadn't. The place is trashed. The floor is covered in junk, the seat is up on the toilet and it looks like barf in there. The mirror's missing off the wall except for one jagged corner and the sink has something spilled in it that I decide not to guess about. I want to leave, but I have to pee so bad.

I go over to the paper towel thing but a course there're none. I look for toilet paper and I see a roll hanging on an old nail where maybe a picture hung in better days. I reach up and take it down, looking it over real careful for mess or bugs. It seems all right so I unravel some and use it like a mitten to knock down the toilet seat. It falls with a bang and even though I was the one who made it fall, I jump like I'm scared. I am a little scared. This place is spooky and nasty. I want Momi to be in here going on about how people live and cleaning it up all along.

I roll more toilet paper onto my hand, reach over, wipe off the seat and throw my paper mitten in over the whole mess in there. After that I stand and try to decide if flushing it before I sit would cause more problems I don't want to deal with, because squatting over that mess is a scary thought. I have to pee so bad that I can't think on it long, so I just pull down my pants and hold myself off the seat with my leg muscles. I keep my eyes up off the floor because I don't want to see anything to freak me while I'm trying to pee.

The paint is cracking off the cinder blocks and someone has written nasty in black spray paint. I'm still holding the roll, so I get a wad ready. When I wipe though I see something I was not ready for: blood.

I jump up away from the toilet like it's the can's fault, and look again at the wad in my hand. Blood. Brownish-reddish blood. I throw it in the toilet like it's hurting me and lean over to look in my pants, and there sure enough is a big stain like the water mark on my bedroom wall under the window.

I stare at it. It's not like I don't know what it is, I do. Monica got her period a couple months ago and she told us all about it and everything her big sister taught her. Xoshell was so jealous she pretended she already had hers, but everybody knows what a big liar Xoshell is so we all just ignored her and got Monica to tell us more details about it. Monica said her sister showed her how to put a tampon up there. First she tried to do it herself, but she couldn't get it in with her sister yelling through the door, "There's only one hole you need to be worrying about." We all laughed at that part of the story. The word *hole* seemed so funny. The whole thing seemed real funny at the time. Now it's not too funny. It's scary and I feel dizzy and like I might throw up.

I reach out to steady myself and my hand gets in the junk poured in the sink. I pull my hand back and scream like I've been bit. My legs start shaking and I don't know what to do standing in this nasty room with my pants down and blood coming out of me.

The Lord is my shepherd comes into my mind. It is Momi's voice I hear. Momi's voice, I want to hear Momi, I want her right now. I need Momi. And before I know it, I am crying. I lean back on the door not even caring anymore about all the mess. I want my Momi. I want to go home and come out of the bathroom and see Momi sitting on the couch watching TV and go over to her real slow and say, "Momi, I'm a woman now." That was part of Monica's story but I make it part a mine.

I can see Momi's face exactly, how she would turn her attention from her show to me and I would say it again and she would take a minute to think on what I meant and then she would light up about it. "Oh baby," she'd say reaching up and pulling me down to her. We would cuddle like that for a bit while she told me all the secrets and I smelled her strong Momi smell.

Knock, knock. "Kianna? You in there?" It's Uncle Luis's voice and I am startled out of my crying, feeling caught and scared again. I reach down and pull up my pants then look around for the roll of paper I must've dropped when I was crying.

"Kianna?" His voice sounds nervous.

I stuff a big wad of paper down my pants between my legs. "Yeah?"

"Oh good. Uh…."

"What?"

"Edgar in there with you?"

"What?"

"Edgar, is he in there with you?"

"No! Course not!" What does he mean about that? I want to wash my hands so I try the faucet. At first there's nothing and then there is a great burst and brown stuff sprays out.

"What?" Uncle Luis sounds alarmed and I realize I musta screamed.

I pull open the door so Uncle Luis will see part of what I've had to deal with, but he just says "You seen Edgar?"

"Edgar?" I am confused. The darkness is making me blind. I feel the brown stuff dripping off me onto the floor, and the wad of paper sitting like a Subway sandwich between my legs, and Uncle Luis is asking me again about Edgar.

"Yeah, Edgar. What's wrong with you?" And if he didn't sound so impatient and a little mad, I might tell him.

Instead I shrug.

"He's gone off," he says and I begin to understand.

I push out from under the weight of the door I have been holding open, out into the night, which feels cool and refreshing after that bathroom. I walk over to the car with Uncle Luis on my tail and try to open the door, but it's locked. I look in the passenger window.

"He's not in there," he says.

Duh, of course he's not in there. I'm looking for his stuff, and I want to cry again when I see it's not in there. This night is so bad.

I lean on the door with my head back, my face up to the sky. I try to keep the tears in, but they roll out anyway. First Popi, then Momi, now Edgar has left me.

What have I done so bad? What is it they all had to get away from? I want to know that. I sniff and wipe my nose on my sleeve. When I do, I feel that it is already wet and I remember the sink and feel glad it's dark out. At this point I don't want to know what I just wiped on my face. I turn my head and wipe it again on my shoulder.

Uncle Luis is still standing there. Does he think I know what to do? I'm just the kid, not even out of fourth grade yet, just months past a decade old. He's the grown-up man all educated and owning a car. He's supposed to know what to do. Suddenly I want to punch him. Make him do something even if it's to bend over and hold himself.

Tires screech and lights come around the corner fast. A couple people scatter and then holler after it when it drives away. In the streetlight, I can see their gestures and hear their cursing. Then before they're even done another car comes fast following the first. It almost hits one of the people and swerves in our direction. I hear a shot and see the man who was almost hit has a gun in his hand too. I duck down behind the car then and pull Uncle Luis down, who is in some kinda shock.

"We gotta get out of here," he says in a whisper, reaching up to open the passenger door.

"Not without Edgar we're not," I say out loud.

I hear the second car backing up, then revving up and taking off. I hear shouts like the car's gone after the people. Uncle Luis is jiggling with his stupid car key to get open the door, then climbs in, pulls at my arm to get in the car and I do, then another shot and the sound of glass breaking. I pull the door closed behind me without sitting up.

Uncle Luis slouches down in the seat, sliding himself behind the wheel and putting the key in. He starts the engine.

"Hey," and I think it's me that said that, but then I hear it again and I peek up to see the man with the muscle mountains calling us from the station door.

Uncle Luis peeks up over the dash enough to see where he's going and pulls out fast.

"Hey!" The guy yells one more time and I figure it out then. I didn't give the key to the disgusting bathroom back.

Uncle Luis tears outa the gas station lot and goes down the street the two cars came out of. This doesn't seem too smart to me, but I don't say nothing. This is all so messed up it's making the bathroom seem normal.

I look out the back window and see that it is partly missing. That broken glass sound was our back window and even in the dark, I can see the pieces shining as we pass under streetlights.

Uncle Luis is driving too fast, putting ground between hisself and trouble. If Uncle Luis gets arrested, he's the last one I got.

"Slow down," I tell him and I hear my mother's voice.

He doesn't say anything, but he right away slows down some.

I shift in my seat trying to get comfortable on the paper in my crotch and look up to the sky for some answers. It is totally cloudy up there, not one star for me to look at and I think of Edgar. I squint my eyes to make them show up, like they're there instead of all those clouds. I want to see the bunch that make a spoon that Edgar says is the Big Dipper. Just now I want it to reach down out of the black sky and scoop me up. Take me away from this lost feeling.

Chapter 8
New York

This is the longest I have ever driven and as day drops into night I feel an odd sensation come over me. I've become removed from the gas pedal, the steering wheel, the numbers on the dashboard, the signs along the highway. I am even removed from the kids on the seat next to me, their voices and the voices on the radio. I am more a thought than a man.

When I let myself continue to go into this crack between day and night, I feel a sense of freedom. Being neither here nor there, not day, not night, everything seems beautiful. I have a feeling of rightness. All the questions fall away and I am still. Each breath I take fills me and I expand, growing bigger. Not bigger in body, just bigger in self.

If this keeps up, I might not need the cassette tapes I've brought along. I have entered a relaxed state without planning to. Something unplanned has happened and it is pleasant.

Watch it! A car swerves in front of me and I brake to keep from hitting it. I look over but the kids don't seem to notice. I look back to the road and realize that I don't know where I am. I was so expanded and then came back so fast that I feel confused. I ask for my directions and then Kianna points out that the gas light is on.

We have to get off for gas and I wonder how long that light has been on and am cursing myself for not noticing sooner. Part of my efforts to take better care of myself means keeping better track of details. At home I have those details down, but now that I've left Springfield, there are unexpected new ones emerging. Gas is now one more detail I will to add to the list of what to keep track of to take better care.

When we get off the highway, I see that we are in a bad part of the city and I want to find a station right away and get back on the highway, but of course there is nothing around. I flip my lights on. The next one after the burnt-out station is in a rough neighborhood and I reach back and lock the back doors when we all get out. Kianna runs to the bathroom and Edgar gets out stretching and looking around.

"Lock your door. And stay by the car while I go in and pay for the gas," I tell him.

He doesn't answer, but he rarely does so I head toward the station.

The booth is lit up making the outside seem darker than before. Inside, the man behind the counter has a six-pack like nothing I've ever seen before. His face has a rough look, but he smiles at me when I come in and I smile back. Right then I know he knows me, and I wonder if he is the same.

"Twenty dollars worth, please," I say, handing him the money.

"On number two?" And I can see he is trying to make conversation because mine is the only car out there.

I smile at him again.

"You from around here?" he asks.

"No." I begin to tell him where I'm from, but then I think better of it and change my game. "You?"

"Thirty years," he nods.

I wish I had asked for fifteen dollars' worth so he could give me change, but I didn't so I turn to leave.

"You need a place to stay?" he asks as I reach the door.

"I got kids with me," I say.

"Where?"

And with his question, I look out the big window to see Edgar is not by the car.

"One's in the bathroom," I answer.

"That little girl yours?"

"My sister's," I say, looking around for Edgar. "Thanks," I say as I pull the door open.

Outside I look behind the station to see if Edgar is waiting for the bathroom, but he's not there. Maybe there are two back there and he's in the other one.

I go back to the car and begin to pump the gas. The ripe smell of it opens up my sinuses and I turn my head away, careful not to pull out the nozzle and spill it on my shoes. I hate the smell of gasoline. It brings back terrible memories of being a boy and the things kids did with it.

I see some figures begin to gather across the street, hoods over their heads or backwards caps, just their silhouettes visible in the dimming light. I don't like the looks of it; it's like something's about to happen over there. I begin to count by threes in my head. This is something I've done since I was Kianna's age to help in stressful situations. It seems to calm me or at least distract me.

Thirty-nine and the gas clicks off and I look to see the numbers on the pump turn to two, zero, zero, zero exactly. That's satisfying. I hang up the nozzle, screw the cap back on, then flip the lid and head over to the bathroom.

"Kianna? Are you in there?" I ask after knocking. She doesn't answer me and I knock again. "Kianna?"

Then I hear her voice. "Yeah?"

I want to ask her if her brother is in there, but suddenly that idea seems preposterous.

"What?" she asks. Her voice is very small.

I look around the back of the station and the neighboring parking lot, but there is no sign of him, so I ask. "Have you seen Edgar?"

"What?"

"Edgar, is he in there with you?"

"No! Course not!" She sounds insulted and then she screams.

"What?" I call to her.

The door opens and she stands there with such a look on her face, blinking at the darkness I'm standing in. I ask her again if she's seen her brother. She seems confused, rattled even. I ask her again, but she can't put two words together, looking over my shoulder into the night. This is the longest time I've ever spent with her and I begin to realize that I don't really know her at all.

"He's gone off," I tell her.

She goes past me to the car and looks for him.

"He's not in there," I tell her.

She whirls around and leans up against the car just staring and that's when I hear sounds from across the street. I look to see what the disturbance is just as a car comes out of nowhere. Another car comes after it and then from across the street come gunshots. Kianna and I duck down instinctively.

"Get in the car," I tell her, trying to open the door. It won't open and I feel a panic rising. I pull the keys from my pocket and jab at the door lock feeling angry that being safety conscious may jeopardize our safety.

Kianna protests about Edgar, but when I pop the door lock open and climb in across the seat, she gets in anyway. I begin to count in my head again; this time it requires a more complicated number so I choose sevens.

There is a crashing sound and Kianna and I duck down in the seat. The rear windshield of the car has shattered into pieces raining into the back seat. Without thinking, I start the car. Kianna slams her door and we are off like a rocket out of that scene. The muscle man comes out as we take off over the curb.

I drive away from the action into the darkness of Harlem.

Some places are lit, but some are not. Kianna tells me to slow down and I realize I am racing. My heart is racing. I turn the car lights on. Where is Edgar? The shattering of the window interrupted my sevens and I can't remember where I was. I begin automatically at 49. That's the rule when you drop count; you start at the square or the cube of the number, whichever is closer.

The first drops splat on the front windshield like spit from an upper floor apartment, but then they come faster until it is pouring. I have no idea where the switch for the windshield wipers is and I start pushing buttons and turning knobs. The hazard lights begin to flash and the turn signal ticks and then finally there are the wipers, knives leaping up and clearing the water away. I begin counting sevens to the rhythm of the wipers: *sixty-three, seven-ty, seventy-seven, eighty-four, ninety-one….*

Kianna rolls over into the back seat and begins throwing things up front.

"What are you doing?" I ask her.

"Keeping stuff dry," she calls. The rain is coming harder and is loud on the car roof.

I look in the rearview mirror and see the rain coming in the back windshield. "Be careful of all the glass!" I yell so she can hear me over the sound of the torrent on the metal roof.

She hurls herself back over the seat into the front holding her backpack. "We've got to find Edgar," she says plainly.

Up ahead I see the light of some store. I pull up in front of it. It's a Rite Aid.

"First we have to tape up the back window or there will be a flood. You stay here. I'll be right out," I say.

"I don't want to stay here. I want to come in with you."

"No, I want you to stay in the car," I say, trying to make my voice sound firm. We are yelling at each other over the rain even though we're sitting right next to each other.

"No," she says, opening her door.

"Kianna," I start.

She slams the door and runs into the Rite Aid. I get out and follow her, the rain soaking my head before I even reach the store.

The lights are surprisingly bright and I don't see Kianna anywhere, though I know for sure she came in here. I can't lose them both. I'm not ready for this kind of responsibility. This is exactly why I told the Department of Social Services no to begin with; they're too much for me.

I want to call out for Kianna but the woman behind the counter frowns at me dripping at the door. I think I might faint from the stress. Instead I turn away from her and head down the medicine aisle. *Focus on the task at hand* I repeat to myself from my mindfulness tapes. *Be in the now.* Now I am looking for duct tape and a big sheet of plastic. Focus: What aisle would those be in? I get to the other end and look at the block letter signs hanging over each row. Maybe "gift wrap," or no, "hardware." I'll try hardware.

The row has so little hardware, it is ludicrous. No duct tape, but there is a blue tarp for camping. I pull one off the rack and head back to the end of the row to review the signs. When I do, I see the edge of Kianna's red tee shirt rounding the corner. I follow her until I see we are in the women's aisle. I stop and watch her. She is looking hard at the products. She slows and then stops and really studies the shelf before her.

What's true is that I have no idea how to relate to a ten-year-old girl. She'll be better off with her grandmother in Florida, where she can have a real life. She can do what girls do, and frankly I'm not even sure what that is, what girls do.

I return to the end and read the signs. Maybe "gift wrap" after all. Aisle three. I find it and pass through images of balloons and streamers, babies and wedding bells. I stop and look at all the cheerful gift bags and wrapping paper, curled ribbons and metallic bows. It all looks good to me. I want to buy a little of it all and paper the car. Wedding bells on the windows, bows hanging from the rearview mirror…. Then I remember the rear window and continue down the aisle to the packing section.

There beside the little padded envelopes is a thick roll of clear plastic tape. It's not duct tape, but it will do. I take it and head down to the cash register to pay.

"Come on Kianna," I call to her down aisle seven as the cashier puts my things in a plastic bag.

She startles, but comes along stiffly.

At the door I prepare myself to be wet again. I look down at her. "Should we buy a box of garbage bags?"

She shakes her head. "Let's just go."

She is acting strangely. A way I have never seen her before. She's probably worried about Edgar.

"Here we go then," I say, holding the door open for her. We both race to the car and jump in our sides, closing our doors—hers, then mine.

I take off my glasses and wipe my face with my sleeve. Then I use my shirt to clean the lenses and put them back on. I open the Rite Aid bag in my lap. "Okay, it's time to do some repairs." I look in the back to check out the damage. It is too dark to really see. When I turn back Kianna is wrestling with her backpack.

"What're you doing?"

"Nothing," she says real fast.

"Put that away, we have work to do."

"I have to use the bathroom," she says.

"The bathroom? You just went a few minutes ago."

"Yeah, well, it was gross in there and I couldn't really go."

"Oh." I hadn't thought about that, but it was a broken-down place. "Okay, let's just get this tarp in the window first."

"Okay," she agrees.

I don't want to go back into the rain, but climbing over the seat doesn't really appeal either. I sit thinking.

Kianna flips over the seat. "Come on then," she says, impatient.

"All right," I say before flipping over, careful not to kick her. I land on the side with glass all over the seat. "Ow!"

"Did you get cut?" she asks.

"I don't know, I can't see." I hold my palm out to try to get it in the streaks of street light, but still I can't see a thing.

"Where's the stuff?" she asks.

"Oh right." I reach back over into the front and feel around for it.

It takes longer than I thought it would, but finally the tarp is stuck up there, crooked in a way that disturbs, but with enough tape to keep the rain out. I used the bag to wipe the glass onto the floor. We wait for the downpour to let up, sitting on the backseat like passengers.

An odd calm has come over me. All the adrenalin of the getaway has drained into my wet loafers and the wet of my shirt feels warm. I know I'm in a car that was just shot at with a strangely silent niece in a dangerous city I don't know and that this should be disturbing, but I feel nothing. Kianna seems oddly quiet and distracted. Maybe she feels the same empty feeling, but I'm surprised she's not more upset about Edgar's absence.

The rain slows and then we both get out the side doors and stray pieces of glass fall into the water on the street. I want to reach down and collect them, but force myself into the front seat.

It's time to find Edgar.

I turn on the car engine and do a U-turn, heading back up the street we came down. With the rain letting up I could turn down the wipers, but in this old car there are two settings; on and off. I decide to have them off and use them every block or so to keep the windshield clear.

The gas station on the corner looks quiet enough as we pull up to it.

"You're going back here?" Kianna's voice sounds doubtful.

"I thought Edgar might have come back to look for us, or at least for a roof, when the rain opened up."

I pull into the station, but instead of parking at the pump, I drive right up close under the dim light of the station. This will be better in case of action or weather, or both.

"Wait here," I tell her, but this time she doesn't even talk back, she just gets out without speaking to me. She pulls her backpack out and hoists it over one shoulder.

"Where're you going?" I call after her. She ignores me and I get out too and watch her round the station towards the bathroom. "I thought you said that bathroom was a dump?" But she is already around the corner, the back of her shirt darker red where her wet hair has been draining. I hardly understand a thing she does anymore.

I am torn between following her and this fear of the darkness that is rising in my throat.

My eye catches motion from inside the station, and for a moment I think it's Edgar. But then I look closer, my glasses being a little misty and I see that it isn't him at all, but muscle man. What was Edgar wearing when he took off? I know he had on that white tank top earlier. Did he put a shirt on over it after that? What color was the shirt he had tied around his waist this morning when I picked them up? Was it really only this morning that we began this whole thing? It seems like days ago by now, though I remember clearly the morning dawning blue, waking up happy, almost excited, whistling while pumping gas into my new red car on the way to pick them up. Then feeling a little sick driving up Pine Street to get them, remembering why we were going on this trip, remembering that Callie was dead, that I would never see her again, or hear her voice call out to me from the window of the apartment.

The shirt was black. I'm pretty sure it was funeral black; I remember even thinking that as he complained about the heat and tied it around his waist before we left. I thought at the time he was trying to cover up his feelings about leaving the place, feeling sad about everything that had happened, but maybe he really was just hot. He did have sweat on his brow above his carefully shaped eyebrows and his hair glistened with gel so he was shiny on two fronts.

Kianna looked small and scared in her red tee shirt and short jeans. I thought at first she must not have had new clothes since last spring and hers were just too small, but she's a quick one. She saw me looking.

"They're called capris and they supposed to be short," she said, giving me fashion news.

Then we all three just picked up the bags at the door and went down the hall to the stairs. The neighbor stuck her head out.

"*A dónde vas?*" she asked in a mean voice. Where are you going?

"Miami," Kianna answered her.

"Miami? *Es que una tienda?*" She asked thinking it was the name of a store.

Edgar snorted, but Kianna answered kindly, "*No, la señora Pérez, que es un lugar. Es un lugar en la Florida. Nos estamos moviendo allí.*" No, Mrs. Perez, that's a place. It's a place in Florida. We're moving there.

This much Spanish I know, especially since Miami and Florida stick out like elbows, but then they got into a more complicated conversation. Mrs. Perez disappeared into her apartment, and I thought we were done and began to move toward the stairs again.

"She's getting something," Kianna said.

"Oh," I said and waited with them to see what it was.

Soon Mrs. Perez showed back up at the door with a small picture of Jesus and a bunch of plantains. A few more words were exchanged, during which Edgar was silent, until Mrs. Perez grabbed him up in an embrace.

He patted her shoulder. "*Gracias Tito*," he said, and I was surprised by his respect for her.

Kianna held her around the waist with both arms and Mrs. Perez hugged her back, whispering more Spanish in her ear. Kianna finally pulled away, crying. She picked up her bags and walked away in front of me without looking back.

"Thank you. *Gracias*," I said awkwardly, and then shuffled down the dark hall behind the kids.

Remembering this early part of the day makes me see how Kianna has changed as the day has gone on, becoming her brother, barely speaking now.

"You're back," muscle man says, sticking his head out of the station, flashing a quick smile.

"Yeah, they shot out my back window," I say, gesturing to the car and my sad repair job.

"That's the Welcome Wagon for you," he says still smiling.

"Have you seen a boy?"

"A boy?" He squints his eyes.

"Yeah, my nephew. He's tall with short trimmed black hair. Have you seen him?" I try to keep the worry out of my voice.

Muscle man is looking past me. "That him?"

I turn around to see the shape of a man coming towards the station. The way the lights are I can't much make out any more than he's carrying something on his back. Just then I hear Kianna scream from around back. I run with my heart pumping around the side of the station and I see both her and Edgar there. He is trying to calm her, but she can't seem to stop herself from screaming.

"Kianna!" I yell.

Her screams ring out into the black night. Her eyes are big and her face is stark white.

I grab her by the shoulders and give her a little shake. No response, just screaming. In desperation I clutch her to me, pressing her face into my wet shirt.

"Shhhh, hey now, shhhh," I shush her and rock her like she is her mother on a bad trip. In a minute she stops the screaming. I keep holding her to me as the sound slowly fades into the dark.

"What happened?" I ask Edgar, who looks about as shocked and scared as I feel.

"I don't know, really, I…don't know."

"Where were you?"

"I was in the bathroom changing my shirt, and when I come out, Kia was here and she jumps back and starts all that screaming, like I was after her with a knife." His voice shakes, and I can tell by the plain way he talks to me and by using her old nickname, that he is really undone by all this.

"Okay, okay," I say, soothing them both, or maybe even all three of us, the best I can. I stroke the back of Kianna's hair the way I used to do with her mother when she would have one of her cries.

I just want Kianna to stop shaking, to look up at me normal and be all right.

"Kianna?" I say real gentle. But she doesn't move off me. "Kia?" I say again, this time pulling her shoulders back from me so I can see her face. She is a lead weight, her neck bent, her head flopping off me to face the ground.

This is not good.

"Was she in the bathroom?" I feel confused about the events.

"Nah, I was in there," Edgar tells me.

"You didn't see her, or talk to her until she started screaming?"

"No," he says, shaking his head to be sure I'll believe him. "Well, yeah," he quick changes his story. "I heard her, well I didn't know it was her, but I heard her rattling the handle and I hollered 'back off' thinking it was one of them ugly Crips wanting to take it to the curb."

Kianna's head hangs down and when I let her go she falls back into me, saying nothing. Edgar's words circle me, but I cannot make sense of them.

"What Crips?"

"Them niggers cross the street," he starts.

"Don't use that language," I say, my tone more harsh than I meant.

"Shut up," he says and I want to hit him. "I'm trying to tell you those boys were after me. They're dressed in the Crips colors and they wanted a piece a me."

And even through my anger, I see that he is about to cry. He looks like the boy he really is, fourteen and never been out of his hometown.

I reach out and squeeze his shoulder. He quick shrugs me off, picks up his bag and walks away.

"Where are you going?" I call.

He doesn't answer and I'm about to tell him to get back here, but then I find I am just too worn out. I tip my head back to the heavens for help. Small drops of rain begin to fall on my face. They are like tears there. Then the drops start to come harder. It wasn't supposed to rain until tomorrow.

"Come on." I steer Kianna around towards the front of the station and she moves like I imagine a sleep-walker must move.

When we get around the corner, I see Edgar has gotten into the back seat and he is beginning to lie down. I hope we got all of the glass off the seat back there. I open the front passenger door and lean Kianna in and onto the seat there. She flops down into the seat with her head leaning back, her eyes closed. I careful-ly lift her legs in and close the door. She immediately slumps down onto the door, her wet stringy hair cover-ing her ashen face.

"Everything all right?" Muscle man has come out of the station.

"Yeah, sure," I say trying to sound cool and in control. "These here are my kids," I say, gesturing to the car as I cross around to my side of the car. "We're all set." I don't want his attention now.

"Okay." He leaves that one word behind and goes back to the front office.

I stand for a minute in the rain looking at my wrecked car with my wrecked people feeling Day One has been a miserable failure.

Chapter 9
New York

He just be standing out the car in the rain like a boxhead. I wish he'd hurry up and get in and get us outa here before that crew across the street come round looking after me. The cut in my side throbs and the wad of toilet paper keeps sliding off when I move around.

Get in the car! I want to get out and throttle him for standing there like nothing. I tell myself I'm not hiding lying down on the seat like this, it's my cut aching, but still I wish we'd get outa here.

Feels like hours go by before the boxhead moves into action. Then, just as he's about to pull the handle on the door the big baldy comes out the station and says something to him. He stops, says something back, but then finally opens the door and gets in the car. He fumbles for the key, looks over at Kianna all lumped up, looks back over the seat at me where I lay still as a dead man, and then finally he starts up this heap a junk.

As we pull out the station, I can't help myself and I sit up to look out the back at the Crips. It's total dark where the window was and I just stare at it. My brain is trying to make out why I'm not seeing out the back window. Between the dark and the sound of rain on the roof I feel confused and just lie back down again.

Goodbye, losers. Mess with me. Take my stash. Cut my side. Good thing I got basketball reflexes or I'd be on the street just now, bleeding out in the rain.

The rain. I close my eyes to the sound of it, to the idea of me in the gutter. They was messed up, man. I shouldn't a never gone over there looking for a light. I should a seen how geeked out and desperate they were. The scene plays over in my head.

"Yo, you got any a that hot fire weed?" The ugly one with the scars on his face asked me when I asked for a light.

"Nah," I lied, reaching for my chains, to feel them there, the way each link makes a bump as it fits to the next.

"You a liar." His man with the do-rag closed in on me, the black skin of his forehead shining under the streetlight.

I didn't say nothing then.

"Give it over," Scar face said.

"I'm just looking for a light or something, but I see you boys ain't got one," I said, backing up to go.

"Where're you going, Shorty?" Another one, big chest and red eyes, closed in from the other side.

"Give it over," Do-rag said, pulling out and clicking open his switchblade.

I jumped back almost clear as he goes for me. I didn't even know he cut me till later because what went down next surprised us all. A car fired down the street and comes at us. We're so surprised, we stood there till it comes clear at us. Then we scattered. Scar face took out a gun and fired it at the car. Then another car comes and I crawled over behind an old stinking dumpster. I heard another shot, but I just stayed there holding my bag on my chest, leaning up against the dumpster.

My ears are perked up real good then, but I can't make out all that's happening and then it goes quiet. It smells like crap, like somebody took a dump right close, but I still crouch there. I hear the boys rallying and it sounds like one of them is down. I hear Do-rag swear and something else. Then they're getting the hurt one outa here, probably Red Eyes, and I bet they're carrying him together. I sit tight for a long time, even when it begins to pour.

The rain makes the smell way worse and when I can't take it anymore I puke. I figure they're long gone enough not to hear that. After a little longer I look out and see through the rain; they flew.

I hate to be wet. Always have. Even if I get my sock wet I can't take it, makes me freak all over. Somehow though being totally wet isn't as bad as that.

When I make out for the gas station, I feel the pain in my side for the first time. I reach down and hold it until I get to where Kianna went into the bathroom. The light is coming out the crack.

"Kianna?" I call.

Nothing.

I push the door in a little. It's heavy, so I push it harder. It's empty in there. I look over at the pump and see the car is gone. I can't believe it. I can't believe they took off on me like that. What's the deal?

In the bathroom I see it's been somebody's dumping ground and nobody's been after it with a scrub brush in too long. I see the key on a block a wood on the edge of the foul sink. I look up in the mirror, but there's not enough of it left to see myself in.

I've never been so glad to stand to whiz in my life. There's blood in the toilet and it reminds me to look at where he got me. My bright white tee shirt is a goner all soaked with blood. I pull it off, roll it up and use it to wipe the cut. It doesn't seem too deep, but it's long, going clear around me back to front. I turn on the faucet and water shoots out. I stick my shirt in it and the shirt goes brown. Brown water they got in New York City. I am definitely not staying here.

I blot my side with the wet shirt and then throw it in the terrible sink knocking the key in with it. My pack is wet, but when I unzip it the stuff inside is mostly dry. I pull out my shirt from this morning and put it on. When I do this my side hurts. I button it up the front careful to get them lined up right. I don't want to look like no boxhead.

Wish I had my boys with me, Brock and Fifty, Jaquan and even Killer Cam, though he can be such a jerk sometimes. We'd show those fools what was what with all their knives and guns. If I lived in this town, they'd have something to worry about.

Revenge makes my face hot. I turn again to look in the mirror before I remember it's not there. It's not there. This hole's got nothing.

I pull up my black shirt and see the cut's still bleeding. Look around for some toilet paper and just when I think there's none, I see it stuck on a nail on the wall. I reach and get myself some, then make a bandage the best I can by tucking in my shirt on that side. Good thing it's dark. I look like a total fag like this.

I want to leave but there's nowhere to go now that Kianna and Luis left without me. I could see how he'd want to unload me after I threw his stupid tape out the window and got in that fight with Kia at the last rest stop. But what I don't understand is how he got her to leave without me. I know she's not still mad about the slap. We already worked that one out in the car and anyway she's not one to hold a grudge like me. She forgives what happens before it's even over.

I stay in there a long time until there's a knock. I think it must be those homeboys coming back for me and I get myself ready to take them. All I got on my side is that they don't know when I'm going to fly out from there. So I build it up, let em wait. Then I go busting out with a big noise, ready to go at them.

I see right off it's Kia. She jumps back and sorta cracks up and starts screaming like I got her with a knife. I know I should comfort her, but to tell the truth she's scaring me bad, screaming like that. Uncle Luis flies around the corner and I let him handle it. I make for the car thinking *gibbous gibbous gibbous.*

Now the motion of the car is making me tired. I gotta get away from this day and crib for awhile.

"Edgar," Luis' voice is annoying and I swat at him, not remembering where I am. "Edgar, wake up."

Where am I and why is Luis waking me up? At first even when I open my eyes I cannot make out where I am. It's like my eyes can't make sense of what they're seeing.

"Sit up," he says.

Then I realize that I am in the car rolled on my side, staring at the seat back. I sit up and feel the pull on my side. I reach down, but the toilet paper isn't there anymore. Probably it's not still bleeding anyway.

"Where are we?"

"New Jersey, at a rest stop with a motel. I got a room already. Help me get your sister." His voice is flat and matter-of-fact.

"What time is it?"

"I don't know. One-something maybe. We'll look when we get in the room."

I get out the car, feeling stiff and tired and go to open Kianna's door.

"Slowly," Luis says, and I see all her weight is up against the door.

I let her fall out the door into my arms and hold her there, even though pain fires through me, till Luis comes round. He opens the door the rest of the way and takes her legs.

"This way," he says, leading me with her legs.

She is freaking heavy for a little kid, and my side is busting. I'm not ready for this and I stumble along behind Luis like a retard.

When we get close up to one a the rooms, Luis tucks her legs under one arm like she's the mail and puts the key into the door lock. The door swings open and the bright lights startle me. I blink and stagger in behind him, laying her out on one of the beds.

Right away, even though I'm blinded and dazed, I can see there are only two beds. "There are only two beds."

"Yeah," he says from the bathroom where I hear him peeing already.

"Where're you gonna sleep?" I ask him, waiting for my turn in the bathroom.

"In one of the beds," he answers.

What the hell? I'm not sleeping with no homo. I go past him coming out and go into the bathroom and close the door. I hear him talking.

"You better get used to this arrangement. We got a long way to go and I don't have enough money to pay for two rooms."

Crescent crescent crescent. I am waking up pissed.

"You can sleep with me, or your sister, or on the floor for all I care," he's going on.

I bust out the bathroom and it feels like that thing where you're doing something again you've just done.

"Where're you going?" he calls after me as I take the door to outside.

I ignore him, mostly because I got no idea. Then I see the car and I know exactly where I'm going.

I know he's watching me get back in the car from the door of the motel room. I slam it real good, and get back in where I was just fine before he woke me up. I stretch out on the seat full and close my eyes.

Right away I see my kitchen, which is wacked because I never thought much about my kitchen before now. I see the cupboards on the wall and the one that has the scratch in the paint on the door showing how it was green before Juan painted it yellow that summer. Something about that scratch always caught my eye and had me thinking about how it got there, what made it, who did it. I pictured different things different days. One morning after a bad scene with Juan and Momi and a piece of glass, I pictured him going for her with a kitchen knife and her rolling out the way so he got the cabinet instead. Kinda stupid, I know.

I'm uncomfortable, like I'm lying on knives and it smells like bad bananas down here. I turn on my side to find a better position. This sucks sleeping in a car. Even though it's May I feel cold, maybe because my jeans haven't even dried out all the way. I look to see if the windows are all up, then lay back down with my knees hanging off the seat so I can be kinda curled up.

My eyes closed again, I see Momi's face, the way she looked the last time I saw her. I've thought on that last time a whole lot a times since a couple a weeks ago. Something about how she stared at me, like she wanted to memorize me, like she was going somewhere. I didn't know that where she was going was heaven. I didn't even think about it. Had other things on my mind, like that scruffy TJ saying to meet him at the park on the way to school to have it out.

I didn't want to fight the punk. Not because I didn't think I could take him, I knew I could easy. Not because I thought he'd get one in before I took him out either. More that promise I made Miss J just the day before.

She had me in there with her window open and those crazy chimes ringing. I got sent up there for spitting through the fence at a fire drill. Like spitting is a crime. Anyway, we were talking on about the streets and what they have to teach me and the school and how she knows the rules in school aren't the same as the rules on the street. Then she gets all serious on me, which Miss J hardly ever does. She leans forward and she says "Do you have the courage to check it out?"

And I'm thinking, did I miss something? Check what out?

Then she says it again, only she can tell I've no idea what she's talking about, so she adds something about nonviolence. She starts out slow, but she gets herself all fired up about some of the greatest leaders of our time and how the way of the streets ain't the only way. Only she doesn't say *ain't*. She says, "It's possible to be a leader without violence."

I swear if I didn't know she was serious I would have laughed out loud at that. But she goes on talking about the courage to not add to the suffering. I'd been thinking about that word suffering a lot anyway so when she says it, it's like a boxer bell going off in my head and I think there must be something to what she's saying.

I've been thinking about suffering because of in church, and how they talk on about Jesus and his suffering. One night when I can't sleep I slip onto the fire escape to smoke some. Sitting out there looking at my stars, all easy, I figure that everything I see is suffering. The bum down in the alley, the crackheads out on the street, the lady screaming across the way, the dog limping

along. It's all about suffering. After that I can't stop seeing people's suffering, no matter how hard I try to forget, no matter how much I smoke. In fact I nearly stop
smoking all together because it makes it worse, not better.

So when Miss J says that word, she has my attention. I decide right there to take her challenge. To see
what it's about to not make more suffering. Which is
what I was sorting out, about TJ and the fight in the
park, when Momi gave me that long stare. We was in the
kitchen and I was leaning against the counter with my
back to that scratch and she was leaning on the other
side up on the stove.

"You got anything for me to sign?" She was always
asking me that in case I was holding back on some discipline letter.

"Nah," I say real smooth.

That's when she gave me that long look. Maybe she
was trying to figure if I was lying to her or not, but I
felt memorized, or studied. Like them water samples we
took out the Connecticut River and looked at under the
microscope, all them little bugs.

"Got to fly," I say, already moving to the door.

"Hey," she calls me back, pointing to her cheek.
"Give it."

And I kiss her there.

"What was that?" she says, playing like it wasn't
good enough.

Most days I woulda smiled but gone on out, but
that day I leaned in and gave her another.

I'm glad I did that.

A car pulls up next to Luis's piece a junk and I feel my heart start to pump, like there's trouble coming. When I peek up out the window though I see it's just a couple a white people finishing up on a date. They're sitting in there kissing on each other with the music up pretty loud for this late.

I lie back down and see out the other window that the sky is clearing and some stars are showing. The song they have on is sad. I know it from the music first, but then I start listening in on the words, *when you think you're on your own in this life, well hang on, when you think you've had enough of this life*, and then I'm just crying. Somehow that song is talking about me and Momi all at the same time, and I think for the first time, maybe that's it. Maybe Momi killed herself. Maybe she felt like this song and she couldn't do it no more.

The music is loud enough that they for sure can't hear me crying, but just in case I put my hand over my mouth. My side is throbbing from twisting around and it makes the tears come harder. Between the pain, the thought and the music, there's nothing else for it.

I cry like that for a long time, till I'm not really thinking anything anymore, I'm just crying.

Then the door of the other car opens and closes. I hold my breath, hear footsteps, heels crossing the parking lot—tap, tap, tap. Soon the car and the music drive away, leaving it dark and quiet. Dark and quiet. And still.

Chapter 10
New Jersey

A man's dark face is hollering down a well and the words are echoing out around his head like smoke rings. Then I am in an overly lit store and I turn at the end of the aisle and see blood on the floor. It's making a trail and I follow it. I see the edge of something around the end of the row. I feel for my glasses, but they aren't there. Is it Edgar? Is he bleeding? I turn the corner and see a patch of red. Kianna. Is it Kianna? "Wait!" I say, but it comes out distorted in slow drawn-out sounds. When I turn the corner the aisle is empty, but then I notice the shelves have these little scenes on them. I look closer; I see miniature people walking about in the scenes. There's one that's a Christmas scene. I reach out slowly and touch the fake snow around the decorated house. It's cold. I pull my hand back quickly and the move wakes me up.

I am in a hotel room in Jersey. I look over to the next bed for Kianna. The bed is made. I sit up fast and listen for her to see if she's in the bathroom. I don't hear anything. I reach for my glasses on the bedside table, put them on and look again at the bed hoping I just missed seeing her there. When she's not there, I get up and go to the mostly closed bathroom door.

"Kianna? Are you in there?" I ask cautiously. I am in my boxers and a tee shirt, having left my suitcase in the car last night. Once we had Kianna in the room and Edgar stormed back out to the car I didn't want to leave her alone. She didn't wake up when we put her in the bed and I worried she would rouse just as I was at the car and begin screaming the terrible scream again. In the face of that, sleeping in my underwear seemed a small price to pay for peace and quiet.

There is no answer from the bathroom. I push the door a little and it opens to show a wet towel on the floor, but nothing else. I pick it up and spread it across the towel rack evenly, smoothing the creases out.

Then I go across the bedroom to the window and look out. There she stands at the car. From the looks of it she's having a fight with Edgar, but if he's still in the car I can't see because of the blue tarp in the back window. Having kids is not easy. I feel exhausted from yesterday and without coffee and a shower I am not prepared to deal with today.

The sky is mostly gray, but there is a cleared part over there where I can see blue. I go to the door to hear how loud they're being so early, and the coolness of the air surprises me.

I can't make out what she's saying, but Kianna is on a tear, so I decide to go out there. I get my shoes from where they are lined up in the closet and take my button-up shirt and pants folded on the crease off of the hangers. In the bathroom I put the shirt on over my tee shirt and put on my pants. Back out in the bedroom I slip my feet into my loafers. Without brushing my hair or my teeth, something I always do before I leave the house no matter what, I go out to them.

"You're lying!" she yells. "You do too!"

Edgar grumbles something from inside the car.

"Yes you do, now get up and give it!"

"Give what?" I try to slip right into the conversation.

"My bag. Edgar won't give it."

I lean in and look at Edgar. He is lying flat out on his belly with his legs bent at the knees and his feet up on the opposite window. His face is turned towards the seat and his eyes are closed. Around him I can see the shine of chips of glass.

I look up at where the window was and then down onto the floor where most of the glass lies. It must have been the angle of that bullet to make the whole pane shatter like that.

Standing here in the morning light of New Jersey makes last night seem far away, almost unreal, like it was a bad movie we watched in the motel before bed. This doesn't explain why Edgar is sleeping in the car, but then I don't know why Edgar is sleeping in the car.

"Why are you sleeping in the car?"

He grunts then turns over and sits up. He looks terrible. His hair is all messed up and he has some dark hair on his lip. His eyes have rings under them and he even has something across his cheek. What is that? Dirt? How did he get dirt on his cheek in New York City?

"My bag," Kianna says like she's waiting for me to hand it to her.

I close my eyes and think back. "Did you look in the front? You did move your stuff to the front when it started to rain in."

"Of course I looked in the front," she says like I'm an idiot.

Then I look at her closely. She doesn't look good either. Her face is so pale and her eyes are heavy-lidded. Her hair is wet from a shower, but that brings even more attention to her face and how drawn she looks. I realize then that we never ate dinner. In fact the last meal was at the rest stop where they broke out in a fight, and I don't think Kianna ate much of her food there at all. There is a lot to keep track of with kids—bags, sleep, meals, moods.

"Let's get cleaned up, change and get some breakfast." I say as I go around to the back of the car and open the trunk with the key. "Here's your suitcase Kianna, come and get it so you can get on some clean clothes."

"I need my backpack," she whines, not taking the red duffel bag I bought her for the trip.

"Come on," I ignore her. "Edgar, here's yours," I say, about to pull his out, and to my surprise it is Edgar who comes for his first. When I see him standing up I feel badly for him. He is covered in nicks and cuts and little bits of glass. "Oh dear," I say.

Edgar looks up at me. "What?" He looks confused and still partly asleep. His fingers are looped through his chains and he has a bit of glass on his chin. I reach up to take it out and he swats at me. "What the hell? What're you doin?"

"The window broke. You have glass on your chin." I put my hand into the trunk and pull out his black duffel bag. "Here. Go clean up."

"I mean it. I—want—my—bag," Kianna says real slow and deliberate like I'm too stupid to understand her.

I take a breath and watch Edgar slump across the parking lot. I know he partly walks like that because if he doesn't his pants will fall down, but there is something else in his walk. Something broken.

"Now! I need my bag right now!" There is such urgency in her voice that I turn and look at her, wet strands of long, curly black hair across her face. What is it with her and the backpack?

I walk around her and open the passenger door. The MapQuest papers are strewn on the floor and the map is wrinkled up on the front seat. I lean in, pick up the papers and begin to organize them. Two of four behind one of four. Three of four is damp and the ink has run, and four of four has a footprint on it and is torn nearly in half. Luckily it's an extra map of Miami I printed at work just in case.

I look up from my project to find Kianna storming away and not towards the motel room.

"Hey! Where're you going? I'm looking for your backpack!" I shout after her, but if she hears me she doesn't show it.

Don't give up before the miracle. Who said that to me recently?

I stand there with my papers watching where she will go. Is this what kids do when they don't get what they want? They leave? Do parents have to deal with this or is it a matter of them being left by their mother? That reminds me of another book Ms. Jones gave me. I put the MapQuest papers on the seat and walk around to the open trunk to look for it. It's called something like *When Kids Grieve.* I carefully reorder the trunk and pull it from the small cardboard box I packed for the trip. Here it is *When There is Loss: Looking at Children and Grief.* Close enough.

I sit on the bumper of the car and silently ask for guidance. Then I open the book in the middle and begin reading: *Loss is a process. A child at this age…*I pause from reading to look up at the top of the page for a clue about what age they mean. The chapter heading is *The Elementary Child.* Perfect. I go back to where I was: *A child at this age needs plenty of time in the anger phase. The loss makes them feel lost and that generates feelings of sadness and anger alternately. Don't be surprised if you find the child becomes more unpredictable in his or her moods. The grief reoccurs unexpectedly over a long period of time and this can feel disorienting. Most elementary age children deal with this by rejecting it. Remember from Chapter 3 what a powerful distancer anger can be.* A powerful distancer. They are keeping me at a distance. Their anger is keeping them safe from their grief. That explains a lot.

I look up and see Edgar at the motel room door. He seems to want something. I give a wave and retrieve my bag from the trunk. I hesitate over Kianna's, not knowing whether to take it out or not. I leave it and lock the trunk, going over to close the passenger door and lock it as well, though anyone would be crazy to steal this rig.

At the room Edgar has gone back into the bathroom, but he must hear me come in.

"Got a razor?" he calls.

"Sure," I answer, laying my case out on the bed and unsnapping it. I take a long look at the order there, breathing it in, enjoying the carefully folded clothes, the shoe bag tied neatly around my extra pair of shoes, my leather case of toiletries. I stroke the leather of the case for a moment before reaching inside for the new, unopened package of razors I bought for the trip. I take it to the door and hand it in to Edgar without opening the door any wider. "Here."

He takes the package from me. "Thanks," he says.

"Are you going to be long? I need a shower," I tell him.

He doesn't answer me, but I'm convinced he heard me.

I go over and look out the window for any sign of Kianna. I don't see her anywhere. My nerves can't handle these kids taking off on me one after the other. *Two four six eight ten....* I hear the tape in my mind: *Breathe in the peace and breathe out the disturbance.*

People are starting to wake up and get going. I see one man loaded down with bags, trailed by a tall woman in a pantsuit and high heels carrying nothing but the smallest purse. Another man has a leash he snaps to his dog's collar before he lets the dog out of the car and they walk to the row of bushes at the edge of the parking lot. It's a little white poodle and seems happy to be out with its owner. "Bemper!" The man calls it away from something it's smelling. What is the point of having a pet?

"All yours," Edgar says.

"Thanks," I say, taking one last look for Kianna. "Keep your eye open for your sister will you?"

"Where she at?" The whole room suddenly smells of aftershave.

"I don't know," I admit.

I turn around to see Edgar is all cleaned up. He's wearing a glossy track jacket with a clean white tee shirt underneath his gold chains and a pair of black pants, probably falling off his waist, but the jacket hides that part nicely. His top lip is clean-shaven and he seems to have shaped his sideburns or something. I can still see the small glass cuts, but only because I'm looking for them. They'll likely be gone by tomorrow they're so light.

"Don't you look sharp."

He scoffs at this and says nothing, rolling his dirty clothes into a ball and pushing them into the left corner of his duffel he has tossed onto the chair.

When I come out of my hot shower the air is steamy and my skin tingles. Alive again. I dry off and dress before I wipe the mirror and inspect my face. It has looked a lot worse. I wipe the lenses of my glasses and prepare to shave. I hear voices from the room. Edgar must have the television on out there. I take long strokes down to my chin and think about what my plan should be.

Knock, knock, knock. "When're you gonna be done? You've been in there forever." Kianna's voice. She came back.

He came back. Now she came back.

Maybe things aren't going terrible after all.

I wipe the dots of shaving cream with a hand towel and collect my clothes off of the toilet seat.

"Now. *I am gonna be done* now," I announce opening the door. I look at her right on. She looks back at me. I feel the urge to hug her, but she's been fit-to-be-tied all morning and I'm not certain that would work out well. "I'm glad you're back. Both of you." I look over at Edgar and smile at him. It feels unfamiliar. I think I need to smile at them more.

Kianna pushes past me and closes the door behind her.

"I'll get your suitcase from the car and you can put on some fresh clothes," I call in through the door.

No answer, but I smile again at Edgar as I go past him out to the car. On my way I say the Serenity Prayer in my head.

The sun has broken through the gray morning. The parking lot looks suddenly beautiful. I look around for the man with the white dog, but they are gone. There is a couple with three kids getting into a car.

The littlest one whines, "Do we have to? Why do we have to?" The older sister pushes him in onto the seat. "Hey! Dolly pushed me!" Who is named Dolly anymore?

"Shut up," says Dolly, pushing him again, so he knocks into the other brother.

"Cut it out!" the brother snaps at the two of them.

I look at the parents packing the trunk, totally ignoring the whole thing. Before they close the trunk they turn to each other. The woman says something. The man kisses her. She kisses him back. They wind their arms around each other behind the privacy of their trunk door. I look away. They deserve at least that. It does make me think, though, that parenting must be better when you're not doing it alone.

I fetch Kianna's suitcase and return to the room, where I knock and she sticks her hand out for it. From there I turn to the task of folding my dirty clothes and packing them into my suitcase.

Edgar lies on the bed Kianna slept in and then made again. He has his arm bent behind his head and his feet with big sneakers hanging off the end of the bed.

"What are you thinking about?" I ask before I can catch myself. I spend the next few seconds kicking myself for opening a doorway that should probably remain closed.

"Breakfast," he answers.

I smile with relief. What was I expecting him to say that the word breakfast has me smiling? Running away again? Killing me? Why do I always imagine the worst out of him?

"Are you hungry?" I ask the obvious.

He nods.

"Me too. Kianna? Are you almost ready?"

With that the door swings open and Kianna comes out wearing a purple velour running suit with a yellow tee shirt showing under the hooded top.

"Don't you look nice," I say. "Edgar and I were talking about getting some breakfast. Did you see anyplace when you were on your walk?"

"Yeah, there was a HoJo's down the way."

"Well then let's hit it!" I say a little too excited. To hide this I go to collect my things from the bathroom.

"Cut it out," Edgar says.

What now? I come out of the bathroom to see Kianna pulling Edgar by the leg.

"Get off my bed!"

"Your bed? What'd you pay for it now?"

"Come on Edgar, just get off."

Is she serious? What is going on with her?

Edgar jerks his foot back, but to his credit he gets up off the bed.

Having won that victory she turns and faces me. "I want my backpack now," she demands.

I shake my head at her before I say, "I don't have it. We must have left it in New York somewhere."

And with the truth out like that she walks right into the bathroom.

My stomach growls and I want to leave now. I am about to yell through the door to her to come out of there when I hear her crying. I look at Edgar and see he's looking at me. He's looking at me to see what I'll do, if I can handle this. I need to read some more of that book.

Her crying sounds so sad that I am pulled to the door. Suddenly my meditation tape runs in my head and I begin following it.

Take a deep breath. Allow your lungs to fill fully, expanding, expanding…. Now exhale slowly, as slowly as you are able. With this motion of the air through you, let all thoughts leave you.

And when all thoughts leave me I see a picture in my mind of Kianna in Callie's arms.

"You miss Momi," I say quietly though the door. Then I see Callie stroking her hair. "Come out and let me hold you," I say even quieter.

To my total surprise I hear the click of the knob and the door opens. Kianna stands there with her face covered in tears looking as broken as I have seen her.

I kneel down right there and take her in my arms. She comes to me and just seems to melt there, more tears coming out of her. I stroke her hair just like I pictured Callie doing. I mutter "There, there" into her hair. We stay like that for a while, tears flooding out of her, all undone. I feel the corner of my eyes stinging. I hold her to me and keep her from breaking apart. After a time she is quiet.

"Here." Edgar is there holding out the tissue box.

I look up into his eyes and I see a person I thought I'd lost. I take the box from him. "Thanks."

Kianna pulls a bunch of tissues out of there and cleans herself up.

Neither of us says a thing about the wet front of my mauve shirt. Ordinarily something like that would've really bothered me and I might even have gone into the bathroom to clean it, or to my suitcase to change it, but today it feels different. It feels more like a badge then a mess.

"I'm starving," I say. "What do you say we go and get ourselves some breakfast?"

Kianna smiles at me. It's not a happy smile, there's still a lot of sadness in her eyes. It's more of a grateful smile.

"Yeah," she says picking up her suitcase, "let's go."

Edgar nods at me and turns to get his duffel.

I throw the key on the night stand and we get out of there, before there's any more trouble. My mind is searching itself to see if I can come up with a single thing she had in that backpack. It's going to need replacing. But now is not the time to talk about that.

"I call shotgun," Kianna yells running to the car, like she knows she'll only get it if she beats him there.

"Yeah, right," he says sarcastically.

"You'll both be riding shotgun," I say, thinking about where we could find a car vacuum to clean up that back seat.

I open the trunk for them to put their bags in while they complain about the arrangement. Then I straighten the bags so they fit next to each other perfectly, like numbers in a column.

Around the side of the car they are pushing each other to get the window seat. I walk around to break it up, and something on the ground catches my eye. I take my handkerchief out of my pocket and use it to pick the item up.

"What's this?" I say, holding up the bloody ball of tissue by its edge.

They both turn to look and their faces freeze in similar expressions, some combination of fear and guilt.

"Well?" I am expecting an answer.

Neither of them says a word. They look away in different directions and even though I know it can't be, it almost seems like they are in it together. What? Did they kill someone and mop up the blood with a tissue?

"What is this about?" I ask again.

Kianna looks like she might faint. Then I think she's going to say something, but she changes her mind and climbs into the middle of the front seat.

"Edgar?" I ask directly.

He looks right at me for a moment. Then he shrugs and gets in beside his sister and closes the door. I hear the sound of the window crank working and then his elbow appears. They are apparently ready to travel.

I want to throw the tissue down onto the pavement and go around to the driver's side leaving the evidence behind. However, my sense of order will not allow this, even in New Jersey. I push my glasses higher up my nose with my free hand and look around until I spot a trash can on the edge of the parking lot. The next chance I get I'm going to look up "secrets" in the index of one of the child development books.

The Howard Johnson's breakfast was expensive and not particularly good, except that it was hot and the coffee was strong. Edgar ate so much food you'd think he hadn't eaten in days and even Kianna put away a stack of pancakes for an adult. I think that means I haven't been feeding them enough and I plan to do better about that. I look at the clock on the dash and figure we'll eat at regular times like regular people, not migrators running away to Florida. Next meal: high noon.

"If you see a gas station with a car vacuum, just call out. I want to get the back seat cleaned up before we leave New Jersey."

"We're in New Jersey?" Kianna asks.

"Duh," Edgar says out of the side of his mouth.

"How long have we been in New Jersey?"

And with this question it seems Edgar and I remember at the same time about last night and how she came unhinged and then went to sleep.

"You fell asleep, and I drove on a bit, out of New York and into New Jersey. We're not that far into the state," I reassure her.

"Oh," she says and then she is quiet for a bit.

The sun is now fully up and there are plenty of cars on the road to keep us company. A lot of sixteen-wheelers pass by, and Edgar starts to give them the "honk" gesture, bending his arm and pumping it like he's pulling a shade down.

Some driver pulls the horn of his rig and it blasts. Both the kids crack up laughing and then they go wild trying to get every truck in sight to do it. I don't understand these kids, especially Edgar. Sometimes he's all withdrawn and acting too old for life and the next he's acting like a total kid, pushing his sister, teasing her or making her laugh. I should probably just enjoy the laughs while they're here.

There's another horn blast from behind so loud it startles me and I jump. We all laugh at that, and the kids spend the next mile reenacting it and laughing. I'm smiling now. Why not? The sun is out, the day is warm, the kids are happy, and we are well fed. I have nothing to complain about.

Chapter 11
New Jersey

I have nothing to complain about. I got what I deserved stealing those pads. Nobody made me do it and now my backpack is gone for good.

I didn't even know we were in New Jersey until Uncle Luis said it about looking for a car vacuum, but then when he said it made sense. What probably happened is we left the city and he carried me into the motel. I wonder if he got blood on him when he did that or if it all ended up in the bed and on my clothes.

When I woke up it wasn't barely light yet and I didn't know where I was but was still in this awful dream. I was in a place I've never been before with Abuela, maybe it was her house that I've never seen before. She was trying to teach me how to dance, and then as I'm moving around I realize I am not put together. That's the best way I can think to explain it, but what I mean is that my hips and the bottom rungs of my backbone were apart from the other part of my bones. I was in pieces and it creeped me out something awful. First, I tried to ignore it, but it was so obvious. Then I tried to hide it from Abeula thinking she'd be mad or upset or disappointed in me. But when I stood straight up I had to fix my bottom part to line up with my top part, the way you fix your panty hose, and it was pretty clear something wasn't right with me. I just looked over at Abuela and shrugged like I didn't know what to do.

I moved to get up, to get outa that dream and then I felt the blood between my legs, looked over and saw Uncle Luis snoring and I started remembering. It began with "Oh yeah, Momi's dead" and then the rest, up to taking the shoplifted box of pads to the gross gas station bathroom. Then I don't remember real clear what happened, but the way I figure it that's where my back pack's sitting right now, outside that disgusting bathroom. I can picture the pink flowers and the key chain collection on the zipper.

Maybe that's God's way of punishing me for doing something I knew was wrong, taking them Kotex. Father Brown as much as told me stealing was one of the worst when he made me do those prayers for the candy bar I said I stole. Maybe it was so bad about the candy bar because it wasn't something I really needed but I really needed those pads. But then God stepped in and I didn't get to even open that box and use a single one, and I lost everything precious to me in the world in the deal. When I realized it was gone I didn't take it too well. In fact since the whole start of the day it was hard to figure out what to do.

First off, I didn't know I could make so much blood without dying and it scared me. I pulled the covers up on the bed so no one would see and get scared like I was. In the bathroom it was a lot worse. The lights were so bright and when I peeled off my jeans and saw how red my white undies had become I felt like screaming. This can't be normal, I thought. I mean I read about it and Monica told us all them funny stories about it, but I didn't expect it to be like that, with real blood dripping out of me.

I took the panties and threw them out the back window of the bathroom into the bushes. Then I stood in the tub thinking so the blood wouldn't get on the mat. I needed those pads in my backpack, which at the time I thought was in the car. I had to get to the car and get the pads and some clean clothes without waking Uncle Luis.

I looked down and saw the spots of blood on the white tub. They looked like the first raindrops on the roof outside my bedroom window, the way they were so alone, but then they spread, and then there's more and soon you can't see the first drops at all anymore. If I'd been less scared maybe I'd have just cried then, but I'm still used to blood meaning you're hurt and I was in a panic.

My mind kept working to calm me down, saying all the facts about how normal it is and all, but the spreading amount of blood was making my heart pound and I couldn't get it to listen to the facts. Then I just took off the rest of my clothes and turned on the shower to wash it all away. I know it really didn't change anything because really I was still bleeding, but it made me feel way better not to have to see the blood there. I turned the water up hot, closed my eyes to it, and started to make my plan.

I'd get all clean, then dry off and quick put Kleenex between my legs before I had to see it again. Then I'd use the blow dryer attached to the wall by the mirror to dry out my pants. After that I'd get dressed and go get my stuff. And that's just exactly what I did.

Wasn't I surprised though when I snuck out there and found Edgar sleeping in the back seat. I was so caught up in what was happening with my body that I didn't even notice Edgar wasn't anywhere in the room. I didn't even remember he was missing.

For a while I just stood there in the beginning light and watched him through the rolled up window. The car was a mess with glass everywhere and the bad job me and Uncle Luis did taping that thing into the back window.

Then I looked in the front where I thought my backpack would be and when I saw it wasn't there I got scared again. There's just no way to get back the things I lost in that pink backpack. I don't care about the bag or the box of pads, though at the time I was kind of freaked out they were gone and I wasn't about to stuff Kleenex in my crotch all day. But then I got some money off Edgar while Uncle Luis was in the trunk and I just went off and bought some more at the convenience store by the motel.

For all I can't stand about Edgar I like that he just gave me money without asking a single question. Just like that. I said "Edgar, *dame chavo.*" And he reached in his pocket and gave me what he had, which was a five. Just like that, no trouble or hassling me over it. He just gave it and went around the side of the car to get his bag from Uncle Luis.

I tried one more time with Uncle Luis, just in case he was being stupid and thought I meant my suitcase. But then I saw for myself he had no idea, so I went and took care of things myself.

The thing is though, not much else in the backpack except for a few books from the church book drive can be replaced. It was all real special stuff. I keep trying to forget about it because there's nothing anyone can do about it, and maybe it really is God's way to get me to learn about stealing, but it's hard to keep my mind off it. I keep picturing things in there, or seeing something that reminds me of something in there. Like a ways back there was this bumper sticker that had one of those Jesus fish on it and a bunch of other ones about Jesus being The Man and all, and I thought about that little laminated picture of Jesus Mrs. Perez gave me. She put it in my hand and gave me a blessing. It was a lost child blessing I recognized from church. Something in that feels like home. Like, now that I don't have it, I don't have my home anymore.

"*Qué pasa con usted?*" Edgar asks me. What's the matter with you?

"Nothing," I say back in English. I don't want to talk in Spanish just when I'm missing something as stupid as Mrs. Perez.

"What were you thinking about?" Uncle Luis asks.

"Mrs. Perez." I tell the truth because I know I've got to make it up to God for what I did with the Kotex.

For some reason that makes them both laugh.

I don't know why, but hearing them laugh makes me feel better, even though they're probably laughing at me.

"What were you thinking of?" I ask Uncle Luis back. He doesn't answer right away and I get the feeling he's coming up with a lie so I butt in. "The truth!"

He laughs again. Uncle Luis is in a good mood today.

"Okay, the truth. I was thinking about your lost backpack and how to make it up to you. Only, I didn't want to say it because I didn't want you to get sad again," he says.

"Well, I was thinking about Mrs. Perez for the same reason, because I was thinking on that Jesus blessing card she gave me and how it's lost forever in my backpack," I say.

"That's a coincidence," Uncle Luis says.

"What's a coincidence?" I ask him.

"It's like something that happens," he stops, then starts again. "It's like two things that happen at the same time when it wasn't planned," he stops again. "That isn't it really. I don't know that I can explain a coincidence. It has some unexplainable part to it."

"Like how we were both thinking about my backpack?" I ask.

"Exactly," he says.

"What is it called when more than two people are thinking about the backpack?" Edgar asks.

I look at my brother and I think he is beautiful. His hair is perfect and he made his sideburns all pointy and pulled out those loose hairs I seen yesterday. Even the pimples are looking better, and the little cuts from sleeping on glass make him look better somehow.

"Hmm." Uncle Luis is thinking.

"A double coincidence?" I suggest.

"I think it's a sign," Uncle Luis says mysteriously, veering off on an exit unexpectedly so as we all tip into each other and the car goes sailing down the off-ramp.

"What?" Edgar asks.

"A sign," Uncle Luis repeats like when he says it again it will make perfect sense.

Edgar and I look at each other, but instead of it being like Uncle Luis is wacked I feel kinda excited.

I hear the blinker go tick, tick and then we turn.

"Why we getting off here?" Edgar asks.

"When you get a clear sign like that, you must act on it right away," Uncle Luis says.

"What are you talking about? You sound like that tape a yours," I say, but I can see he's concentrating. There is somewhere he is getting us to, reading signs and turning.

"Found it!" he calls out as the big sign for Kmart shows up out of nowhere.

Uncle Luis turns in and parks. Maybe he's going to buy a car vacuum. I know that broken glass has been on his last nerve.

"Come on." He gets out all happy.

It's not as hot as yesterday and when we get out and cross the parking lot the breeze feels real nice. This is good because I honestly don't know how soon I'm supposed to change this pad. I figure it'll last longer than a tissue, but I don't know how long that is. I stuck one in each of my pockets this morning, just in case.

When we get in the store I see the sign for the restroom right away.

"I gotta go to the bathroom," I say. "Where you gonna be?"

"Meet us at the register in a couple minutes," Uncle Luis says.

I still don't know what we're doing here, but I'm glad not to be using a nasty gas station bathroom.

I go into the Kmart one and it smells so strong of flowers that I have to cough a little. Somebody has been overusing that floral spray in here. I look around and see a fake arrangement on the side of the sink. It looks cheap and dusty, but it does cheer the place up. Maybe they're trying to get us to think that's what's making the flower smell. People are funny.

The last stall is the farthest away from the door. I take it because I don't want anyone trying to push in without looking and having the latch break open while I've got my pants down. I felt that way before yesterday, but now it's even more true.

Before I look down into my panties where the diaper is laid out I pee and read all the graffiti. Most of it I don't totally understand, but I like the little poem about flushing. I like poems in general. Sometimes I make them up in my head and sometimes I hear ones I read before. They just come up into my mind. Like last night on the way from the store back to that bathroom I heard the line *And miles to go before I sleep* in my head out of nowhere. It's been bugging me to think of what poem that's from. Something famous I think. Anyway I sure didn't read that one on the bathroom wall.

Today there's something different. It says:

Prayer that goes where I go,

Prayer that sees me as I really am,

Prayer that drinks from clear water, lies in tall grass, wishes on stars.

Humble prayer, holy prayer, hold my hand now

When I need to cut my losses, move on down the road

When I need to shed what was and emerge into what is

When I need a prayer that goes where I go.

This poem is real odd, and long for a bathroom wall, but it gives me the strength I need to take a big breath and look down. It's not as bad as in the shower, but it's still awful surprising to see red there. Next time instead of trying to distract myself I'm going to think in my head "Prayer that goes where I go" before I look. That might help with the surprise. Though I'm not an idiot, I know I'm bleeding, so why's it a surprising thing to see it there?

I never changed a pad before, but I'm guessing you have to touch it with your hands. I reach down real careful and start to pull the thing off my undies. It's stuck on there pretty good, and I remember back at the hotel pulling off the slick paper and rolling it on there a few times till I had it lined up right.

Now I'm holding it like a ruler on the flat of my other hand wondering what to do with it. There isn't any little metal box to put it in. If I put it on the floor and someone comes in they're going to think I'm nasty.

Slowly I open my legs and float it into the toilet. I watch it spin around like an empty raft. It makes me think of bath time I used to have when I was little, and that orange plastic raft I used to float around. I'd try to balance the soap on it and the other stuff around the edge of the tub.

I wipe, and because I was thinking about the boat, it surprises me again that there is blood there. I guess this whole period thing is going to take some getting used to.

Out of my pocket I take the fresh pad and unwrap it from its individual pink wrapper. What am I supposed to do with the wrapper? I add it to the raft and the toilet paper. Then I carefully unroll the clean pad onto my undies and to my surprise I get it on there the first time!

I pull up my pants and flush without thinking. Then a dreadful thing happens. The toilet gets jammed up from all my blood and the water starts to fill up the bowl. It's not stopping and the water is going over the edge.

I jump out of the stall and I'm just about to go for help when I realize that then people will come running in and see my mess. I want it to stop, but the water keeps coming out like it won't stop till the thing goes down. I look wildly around the bathroom for something to shove the pad down. The only thing in sight is those plastic flowers. I run over and grab them.

The water in the stall isn't all that deep so I go right in and stick the flowers in the toilet, blossoms first. I ram where I think the pad is stuck and I get it right off. The water begins to turn in a circle again and everything is starting to get sucked down. I'm happy for all of two seconds, until I go to pull the flowers out and I see one is missing. At this same moment I hear the water coming up and over the side of the toilet again, splashing at my sneakers.

There is nothing for it but to give it up and run out all wet crying for help or to push up my sleeve and pull that flower out with my hand. Without going around on it too much I just shove my hand in the swirling pool and feel for the plastic. When I feel it I yank it out and the water goes right away on back down. I stand there with wet sneakers and a bright pink dripping fake flower in my hand and I have got to laugh a little. I can just picture telling this to Monica and Xoshell and Tenise and them at lunch when Mrs. D, the lunch monitor, is on the other side of the room. I can see them, Monica throwing her head back in her big laugh and Tenise putting her hand up over her mouth so her food won't go shooting out. Xoshell I imagine is so jealous she snorts out her nose.

The last of the water is gone and the bowl is beginning to fill up again when it hits me that I won't be telling this story at lunch because I won't be having lunch with my friends ever again. I am moving.

With that I leave the stall. I stick the wet flower back into the arrangement with the rest of them and put it back by the sink. Then I wash my hands a few times until they reek of disinfectant hand soap. Before I go over to dry them I look up at myself in the mirror. Everything has been such a mess that I don't think I've really looked at myself since in the car yesterday.

My hair dried good today, all full and curly. It comes out the best when I ignore it, just crumple it in my hand a few times when it's wet. Momi says that gives the curl its spring to scrunch it up like that.

It's my eyes though that I look at. They look different to me, though I can't say what it is about them. Something about the darkness around them and the way the rest of my face looks next to them. I didn't expect to look any different about this period thing, but I do. If I really look, I can see that I do.

By the time I reach the registers, my sneakers have stopped that annoying squeaking sound they were making the whole way out of the bathroom. I had to stop walking a few times and drag them like I was wiping dog doo off them or something. But that must have helped after all because they've stopped squeaking. Between my wet shoes and this big wad of maxi pad between my legs it's a good thing most of the day is going to be spent in the car.

"You been waiting long?" Uncle Luis looks guilty, but excited at the same time. He has something behind his back.

"Uh, no," I say.

Edgar is standing behind and he's smiling.

"Here." Uncle Luis thrusts a bag at me. "It's for you."

He hands me a white plastic bag with the big red K on it. I reach inside and pull the thing out. I stare at the brand new backpack. It's purple and has butterflies in this glittery way all over it and a zip pocket in the front with the tag hanging off it. My key chain collection is not there. When I open it my picture of Momi will not be there. All my important things will not be there.

I feel my eyes stinging. I don't want Uncle Luis to get the wrong idea, so I just out and hug him. "*Gracias*," I say into his shirt. "Thank you so much."

When I look up he is smiling at Edgar. "Come on, let's get on the road."

We leave the Kmart and the sun feels good, especially on my feet. I am clutching the backpack to my chest and I can feel that it is not empty, but I don't say anything about it yet. I like holding the surprise without talking about it.

We get in the car in the same positions as before, Uncle Luis driving, me in the middle and Edgar in the passenger seat. It feels right and I decide at that moment to let Edgar have the window the rest of the way without calling it.

I hold the backpack on my lap like a prize. It is new and pretty and I like the way it has butterflies instead of flowers. I look from Uncle Luis to Edgar to decide which one of them picked it out.

"What?" Edgar says.

"Which one a you decided on the butterflies?"

Right away I can tell the question makes them both nervous. I want to laugh watching the both a them try to figure out if the butterflies is good or bad, and how to blame the other one if they're bad, but take the credit if they're good.

Uncle Luis turns back onto the highway and speeds up as he goes up the ramp. "I'd say we came to it together, wouldn't you Edgar?"

Edgar nods still with his head cocked looking at me.

I smile a big one, hugging the backpack to me. "Well I love it," I say, and mean it.

They both sigh hard and lean back into their seats. I didn't know I was that important.

"Open it up," Uncle Luis says.

I carefully pull the zip over the curved top of the backpack, not rushing it. This could be the best moment of the whole day and I don't want it going by too fast. I want to remember when I close my eyes tonight in whatever place that is, this moment of pulling the zipper back. I want to remember how it sounds making its unzipping noise, how the teeth look as they part and how the butterflies on the outside sparkle in the sun coming through the front windshield.

"Go on," Edgar says impatient.

"I'm doing it," I say a little aggravated at him for getting into my moment and rushing it, but mostly happy that he's watching so closely.

Inside there are two books, a spiral pad with frogs on the cover, a set of sparkle pencils, and three gel pens: purple, green, and pink. I look at the book covers and see that one is a *Sweet Valley Twins* book I've already read and one is a *Magic Tree House* book I outgrew like three years ago. Under that I see the edge of something else and I pull it out.

"A diary!" I can't help the excitement. It has a little lock and key and everything. The cover is light pink with a rainbow and says *My Diary* in these really fancy gold letters. I touch them with my finger.

"Do you like it?" Uncle Luis has to ask. I see Edgar is looking out the window with a big smile on his face. He already knows.

I hug Uncle Luis's arm. "Thank you Uncle Luis. It's just beautiful."

"I'm sorry I didn't keep better track of your other one last night. Things got a little out of hand for a while there."

"Yeah, it's okay." I watch the trees flicker by and feel the leaving of it. "Thanks for all the new stuff." I take out the green gel pen and the frog pad and doodle on the first page to watch the stream of green come out the tip. I don't want to think about the old backpack with the stolen pads and the memories of Momi and Popi in it.

"Wanna make a list?" I suggest.

"A list?" Uncle Luis asks.

"Yeah. I wanna write something."

"Okay," he says trying to be encouraging but not seeming to have any idea what to make a list of.

"Bumper stickers," Edgar says.

"Good idea!" I'm truly excited about this whole plan. "You seen any good ones?"

"I seen *I love guns*," he says.

"You've not," I say, flicking him with the pen.

"Have so. Right there on the back of that silver pickup."

"Where?" I am doubtful.

"Slow up," he says to Uncle Luis who listens and sure enough right there on the backside of the truck is *I*, then a big red heart, then *guns*.

"That's the stupidest thing I've ever seen. I love guns? What is that supposed to mean?"

"Juan loved guns," Edgar mumbles, but he doesn't look at me.

That shuts me up. Popi did love guns. He worked at Smith & Wesson making guns, putting the parts of them together. Maybe it was being around guns all the time that made them seem not so bad. But I don't want to talk about that now neither.

"Alright," I say writing it down. "We got one." I draw a big number one in the margin and put a circle around it. "I'll write them down and keep count and at night we can each pick the stupidest one."

"There's one," Uncle Luis points. It's real small print so he can't read it while he's driving.

"Move up," I say.

"Slow down, move up," he says, but he's joking. He speeds up. "Can you read it Edgar?" he asks, just because it's out Edgar's side.

"Naw," Edgar says telling the truth.

I lean over him and read it. "*Stop following me. I'm lost too.*" I write it down. "These are all so stupid."

"This was your idea," Edgar says.

"Come on," Uncle Luis kinda likes having a game. "There's another."

"It says…" Edgar starts.

He and I both strain to read it. I act like I can't see it because the words are easy and I want him to keep playing.

"*Vote no on three*," Edgar blurts.

Then we all laugh, partly because it doesn't make any sense and partly because Edgar just read something.

"Your mom would have loved that one," Uncle Luis says.

Me and Edgar stop laughing and just look at him. He stutters then because I guess he wasn't thinking out what he was going to say.

"I mean she would've thought that was funny. She loved numbers, did you know that?" He glances our way when he says it.

I shake my head feeling a real hole inside me where Momi used to be. Edgar looks out the window.

But Uncle Luis goes on. "Yeah, we were in the same math class for years and at the end she was the only girl."

For one thing I can't picture Momi in a classroom at all, never mind a math one, but the thing I get even more stuck on is the idea of them in a math class together.

"I thought you was older than Momi?"

Uncle Luis gets real fidgety then. "Hey look at that one," he says pointing out the front, reading a sticker. "*I used to have super powers, but my therapist took them away.*"

Edgar snorts, but I don't get it. And I don't get how they were in the same class. Then I think about Ramona and how she's in the same grade as her brother Daquan because she stayed back a grade and how them both don't like to talk about it. Uncle Luis must have had to repeat only he doesn't want to say.

I write the super powers one on the list even though I don't know what it means. I skip asking because I want to stay on the subject of Momi.

"What else did Momi love?" I ask.

"Hmmm," Uncle Luis says, thinking. "She loved equations."

"That's the same as liking math," I say.

"Yeah, but she took it into everyday life," he says.

"Like what do you mean?"

Edgar answers, "Like, two more bites a beans is equal to a cookie."

Uncle Luis and I laugh because that is something Momi said.

"Or like, homework plus dishes equals TV," I say getting the idea.

We go on saying Momi-isms until I spot another sticker I just have to write down.

"Look at that one," I interrupt them. "*God is too big to fit into one religion.*" I get the green pen busy, before the car moves away and I forget how it was exactly.

"That's another one perfect for your mother," Uncle Luis says. "She had so many fights with your grandmother about that."

"What do you mean?" I don't usually feel this stupid. Maybe it's the blood dripping out of me that's making me so dumb that I can't understand stuff anymore.

"Your grandmother is a very devout Catholic," Uncle Luis starts.

"What's devout?" I hate not knowing anything all the sudden.

"It's like devoted. She is a very devoted, loyal Catholic who takes her religion very seriously.

"Like Mrs. Perez?" I ask.

"Exactly," he says.

I look down and read the saying again. *God is too big to fit into one religion.* I'm going to figure this one out without asking, blood or no blood. So Abuela is a devoted Catholic and she and Momi would fight about religion and this says God's too big for one religion.

"So Momi thought there was enough of God for more than just the Catholics?" I guess.

"Exactly!" Uncle Luis smacks the steering wheel. "Your mother believed people should have a choice about religion and that all the religions were holy, not just Catholicism."

"Is that why she never brung us to church?"

I thought I was onto it after he whacked the wheel like that, but this question seems to stop him and make him a little sad.

"I think there were a lot of reasons for that," he finally says.

This whole conversation confuses me. I feel like instead of knowing Momi better after what he's been saying, that I don't really know her at all.

I close up the frog pad and shove it into my backpack.

"Ow," Edgar says like I bit him.

"What's your problem?" I ask all nasty because my mood's gone bad. I can feel my sticky pad when I squirm to get more comfortable.

"You," he says, moving away from me closer to the door.

And then, like he knows my whole story, Uncle Luis starts humming this little song Momi used to sing when she was cooking. The song makes me feel like after I organize the books in my classroom, from tallest to shortest. Like it makes me organized.

I take out my new diary and open the lock with the key, which is attached. I have to figure out what to do with the key. If I bite the plastic ring that holds it on then no one else will be able to open it and read it. But if I do that then I'll probably lose that little key and then I won't be able to open it up either. For now I think I'll leave it on there.

Dear Diary,
We are driving along

"What road are we on?"
"295," Uncle Luis says.

Dear Diary,
We are driving along on 295 in New Jersey on our way to Miami. Everytime something good happens and I start 2 feel a little happy I remember Momi's dead and I start hurting all over. It's like I can't get away from it and I'll have 2 be sad the rest a my life.

She's not even here to tell about my first bleeding time. Which is gross. Bleeding between your legs is just gross. And worse I got nobody to tell about it.

So far there's nothing good to tell you, because you're the best thing I got.

Bye 4 now, K

Chapter 12
Pennsylvania

When Kia asked me for money at the car I wasn't awake yet. Don't know what she did with it neither. Not that it was much, just the fiver in my pocket I keep in case I run across a nickel bag on the street.

It was a wacked morning anyway waking up in the car with Kianna hot on me and then Uncle Luis touching me on the cheek. When I got into the bathroom I saw the glass bits here and there and I thought it looked kinda cool actually.

But then when I took off my shirt and saw what was happening with my side I forgot all about it. The gash musta been deeper than I thought because it was all swollen up and red around it. In the shower when I washed it, it burned and I couldn't let the water go right on it because it hurt too much.

Even now I can feel it as we're riding along and I haven't even done anything to it. It's still kinda burning there. I keep my elbow tucked down to protect it from all Kia's squirming. She's all high about her new stuff and taking it all out and putting it back and every time she reaches in there and pulls something out I've got to watch out for her elbow. That girl has some pointy elbows going on.

I want to push her over into the back seat, but Uncle Luis hasn't found a car vac yet and there's bits of glass all about back there. I didn't know that when I picked to sleep there or I would have slept on the front seat. Or maybe on the floor of the room. Maybe that's what I'll do tonight is sleep on the floor instead of making a big thing about sleeping in the car. It just caught me by surprise is all. I wasn't expecting two beds is all.

Miss J says part of my anger is when I'm not expecting something. She was trying to explain it using a car with gears, but I didn't know what she meant at the time. Then I asked one a the boys down at the South End and they explained about how first gear is for starting up and then second, third, and fourth is for when you're really going. Then it made a little more sense what Miss J was saying, about how I'm the kinda person that has to warm up to an idea.

Kia, she's different. She can switch gears like nothing. How she can go from thinking one thing's going to happen right into something else instead and that doesn't seem to mess her up. I guess that's why being in foster care wasn't so hard on her really. She just went along with whatever all was going on.

Me, I need to know the plan and then stay with it. I don't like when people go changing junk at the last minute. That was what really got me about Sonia. That girl would say meet outside the lunchroom then she'd go changing it to no, meet me by the bubbler. Really that was what convinced me that I care for her that I put up with that all the time. I don't usually take that from no one. One a my boys tried that and forget about it.

"How much longer till we get to Philadelphia?" Kia asks Uncle Luis.

"That last sign said Levittown. Look it up on the map there on the dashboard," he tells her.

She reaches for the papers and starts looking. "We're close!"

We're stopping in the city for lunch. Uncle Luis let up on his tight schedule a bit to include some bell we have to see. He got the idea off a truck going by and Kianna got all worked up and they made a plan. I don't even know half the stuff Kianna has in her head and how she knows it. How does she know about the bell he's talking about and what's so big about a bell?

Me, I could care less, but for this pain in my side aching on me. I'm pretty sure it's worse since this morning, but I haven't looked at it since the shower. I'm keeping my eyes out for a car vac place so I can stretch out after lunch and rest a bit. I looked for my stash at the last stop and I musta dropped in in the mess last night. Too bad 'cause it mighta taken the edge off this pain. I just keep fingering that charm a Sonia's and then it don't feel so bad. It's just that I didn't sleep too good in the car last night.

Part of it was hearing that crazy song that stuck in my head like a big wad a gum. It's still going around up there too. Just the words *hold on* though. I don't much remember the rest but the tune is there. That and dreaming about Juan and how he got arrested. I don't really know anything about it, but it's a dream I keep having about how it went down. Every time I dream it it's a little bit different, but it has the same bad feeling to it.

Last night it was all about the guns. I know for real he was arrested for stealing from his job at Smith & Wesson, but I don't know any more than that. Last night though I saw him in the alley behind our old place and he had all these guns tucked in his belt and he was stumbling around back there. Sort of like he was an old rat who lived in the alley. And when the police lights came a-whirling he was scurrying around like he had nowhere to go. It gives me the creeps to think about it. I don't know why I think about it so much. It's not like he was my father or anything. But still I thought he wasn't like that. I thought he wouldn't do something stupid like that. When Momi told us I acted all like I knew already and like I was suspecting it all along but later that night I was out on the fire escape looking to the stars for answers.

Hard to believe those lights are gas and dust that up and collapsed under its own weight. I think about that a lot when I'm looking at them, how even something as far off and amazing as a star is just something that up and collapsed because of its own weight. Also I think about how things aren't how they seem with a star looking so small and cool when really they're so big and hot.

"Reach into the glove box there and get out the maps, will you?" Uncle Luis is looking for direction again.

I push at the latch, which is jammed but then it falls open crooked like somebody's mouth when they've been hit. I reach in and pull out a fistful of maps. What is all this?

"We are leaving our MapQuest directions!" He sounds drunk about it.

"Yipeeee," Kia joins him.

"What one you want?" I ask.

"I think it's called *Southeastern States*," he says.

I look through for the one with two words, two *S*'s. "Here," I hand it out.

"Open it up, will you?" he asks.

The thing is brand new and folded up real good. When I un-fan it, it stretches out in front a me and Kia both.

"Find Philadelphia," he says.

There is a light orange highlighted line all down the coast.

"Hey, somebody wrote on your new map already," Kia says.

Uncle Luis laughs.

"Nah, really," I say, "somebody did."

"It's part of getting ready for any big trip," he says, flipping his visor down to block the sun coming at him and pushing up his glasses.

"You went through and marked all these maps?" Kianna holds up the pile and lets them all drop down into my lap.

"Yup," he says.

"Wow," Kianna says like it's something big.

"So what route do I take to get into the city?"

I look at this thing and all I see is a jumble of lines and letters. Kia leans in closer and traces her finger along his marked path. She stops and I can make out the word PHILA and under it DELPHIA in red letters. She is smart, looking along the path already there. I lean in.

"How 'bout getting over to 202?"

Kia looks at me. We're doing this thing together.

"202? I saw a sign for that. I think it's coming up. Thanks, Edgar," Uncle Luis seems sparked about this whole detour thing.

Kia is still studying the map so I push it her way and lean back. My side is throbbing from leaning forward like that. Best to chill now and watch Philadelphia come on us.

"Atlantic City!" Kianna bursts out. "We're so close to Atlantic City!"

"That's off to the coast right?" Uncle Luis asks her.

Kianna folds the map over so she can zero in on just the section we're in. "It's a straight shot down…." She hesitates, then goes on. "Down 30 I think, or something. Some big thick highway. It's a straight shot."

She turns the map and opens it all up again looking for something. In the bottom right-hand corner she finds it. It's some kinda key. She holds her finger along a black line at the bottom and then flips back up to where she was.

"Less than sixty miles!" she crows. "Atlantic City is less than an hour away!"

Uncle Luis doesn't say anything but he sure knows she wants him to.

I see one on the back of a pickup and read in my head before I say it out: "*Wear a tee shirt. Support the right to bare arms.*" I gotta think about that one for a minute, but Uncle Luis snorts and pushes his glasses up his nose. Kia doesn't let up though.

"Come on Uncle Luis, it's a beautiful spring day and we could go there instead of the city. We live in a city, we know all about that, but Atlantic City, now that would be something."

I don't know what she's talking on. All that about cities and wanting one over the other. Uncle Luis looks like he's having none of it, but he doesn't yet know how to tell her that.

Kia turns to me. "Xoshell went to Atlantic City last summer and she said it was the best trip she ever had and there's a long boardwalk and all kinds of stuff going on and Edgar, there's a beach there!"

She does make it sound pretty good. I lean past her to see Uncle Luis, but he's still locked on the road. He's more like me than Momi and Kia. Uncle Luis likes sticking to the plan, and he already made one change for her thinking they'd see that bell. I doubt he's gonna be able to shift off that now.

"I get the idea we ain't going there this trip," I say easy like it's not a big deal.

Kia's face is messed up, like she got no place for all the things she's feeling.

"Look," Uncle Luis says pointing at a bumper. "Get out your pad, that's the best one yet."

"*Stop or I'll shoot?*" she reads like she doesn't get it.

"Read the little words," he says.

"*The moon. The Big Apple wants you to stay,*" she reads blankly.

I didn't know exactly what it said at first. I figured
Uncle Luis was just getting her mind off the beach, but
maybe that is the best one.

"You know what the Big Apple is, don't you?" Uncle
Luis asks.

"What?" I say even though any idiot knows it's a
circus. I want to keep the conversation going before Kia
gets all disappointed.

"It's a nickname for New York City."

At that Kia folds up the map, not on its creases
neither, and shoves it in the glove box with the others.

"I hate the Big Apple," she says pushing the crooked
door closed a few times until it catches.

"You have hardly been there," Luis starts, but then
he must think again about going there because he stops.

"Here's 202," I say.

"Right, thanks." And for some reason it feels like
me and Uncle Luis are in this together now.

"You gonna write down the sticker?" I ask Kia. "You
missed two now."

Her arms are crossed in front of her, but when I
say that she reaches in her pack for the notebook. On
accident she jabs my side.

"Ow!" I bust out.

"What?" she says mixed mad and bothered.

"Nothin." I move a little more toward the door and
make myself not touch where it hurts. I've got to get
outa this car now.

"What was it again?" she asks.

"What was what again?" I forget what we was saying
before she jabbed me.

"The bumper sticker?" Mad and bothered again.

It's really about not getting to the beach so I just tell her what I remember they said. Uncle Luis fixes them up because I had it a little wrong on both and she sighs and crosses out my way, writing in his.

When I look up I see we are in the city. It's all clean and nice-looking and the people on the streets look like they be flossing, all done up with the women in hats holding fancy bags. One a them is walking a fluffy dog with a big stupid pink bow on its head.

"This is Philly," Luis announces.

Kia is perked up now that there is something to look at besides bumper stickers.

Down the streets we go until he gets to a more regular neighborhood. He pulls into the parking lot of a restaurant that's not fancy, but it's not shabby neither.

"Well, it's a step up from a rest stop," Luis says and we all pile out.

Inside I go right to the men's room and so does Kia in the women's.

There's no one there so I pick up my shirt and look at the thing in the mirror. That way I don't have to bend to look because it's awful touchy now. I step closer to the mirror and see that it looks nasty. The gash is open and there's all white oozing out of there. Then the skin all around it looks to be on fire. I hear the door and let my shirt drop, pretend to be washing up.

"You go already?" Uncle Luis asks.

"Yeah," I mumble, getting outa there. I don't want to see him that's for sure.

I go to the empty table and take the seat on the left by the window. There I can be scoping out the scene while I wait, and my side is protected in case Kia sits with me.

"Can I get you something to drink?" The waitress is fine. I smile at her my big one.

"What you got?"

She smiles back, but only a little, telling me I've got to tone it down. Her red hair is short and put behind her ears in a way that makes you look at her earrings glittering there. She's wearing a black shirt and a tight black skirt that I can't wait to see the back of. She looks at me expecting something. I look back at her.

"A drink?" she says and I realize she musta tole me what they got and I wasn't listening.

"Uh, Coke. You got a Coke, right?"

Now her smile is just right and she nods. Just then Kia slips in the booth beside me and I'm glad I figured it to keep clear a her elbows.

"Hi," she says cheerful, dropping her backpack between her feet under the table. It hits the table leg and makes it wobble.

"Can I get you something to drink?"

"Um, okay. Can I have a Fresca?"

"Sorry, we don't have that."

"A Sunny D?" Kia tries.

"No, sorry, we don't have that either."

Kia thinks then, "How bout a Root beer then."

The waitress begins clicking her pen in and out. "Coke, Sprite, Diet. Those are all the soft drinks we have. We also have milk, orange juice, cranberry juice, or apple juice." Her voice is so smooth like a dance step done right.

"I'll have a black coffee and a tall water with lemon," Uncle Luis says, sliding into the booth on the other side. He must have knocked into Kia's bag because the table wobbles again.

"What's the one you said before apple juice?" Kia asks.

The waitress thinks and guesses, "Cranberry juice?"

"Yeah, I'll have that," Kia says.

When the waitress turns to go I have to lean forward a little to see her and Luis catches my eye.

"What?" I say looking at him.

He just smiles and opens the menu.

Too late for me to see her leave though.

"Order whatever you want. We have some planning to do," Uncle Luis says too loud. I look over and see he's brought in the map Kia folded up wrong.

"What's a Philly Steak?" Kia asks.

"It's meat with cheese," he tells her.

I look over the menu, skipping the top section, which I figured out is usually salad and soups, till I find the word *burger*. I know just what I want without trying to read the whole thing. I like burgers anyway. I look over at the little doodlings in the corners and I wait to put my menu down until the others do. Then the waitress comes with our drinks on a round tray.

"What's this?" Kia sounds scared.

"That's your cranberry. You did order cranberry juice didn't you?" She's saying that to be nice because she doesn't seem confused at all.

"Uh, yeah," Kia says.

The waitress puts the rest of the drinks out and takes our order. The whole time I'm looking out the window though, I want to be staring at her. A kid on a bike rides by wearing a helmet. Then an old couple leave the restaurant and walk real slow down the street with their arms hooked up.

I think of Sonia and how we aren't ever going to get old together. I don't know that I'm going to get to be that old at all.

"Well?" Uncle Luis asks like he's repeating himself and I look up and see that I missed her walking away again.

"I'm not drinking it because it's red," Kia tells him.

"Because it's red?" Uncle Luis can't figure it.

"Yeah, it's blood red and I can't drink something that looks like that," she tells him.

"Didn't you know that it would be red when you ordered it?" He straightens his table setting.

"No!" she says all in his face.

Then I think he understands that she doesn't know about cranberry juice, so he just drops it.

"I thought we'd talk about the trip a little," he says, picking up the map and unfolding it. He turns it to face us. "We are right about here." He points to the map. "In a couple hours from now we will have been traveling for a day."

A day! We've only been going a day? It seems like way more than a day.

"Down at the bottom of this map is Charleston," he says pointing and then flipping the map over, "And then you see it picks up at Charleston at the top here and all the way down at the bottom on this side is Miami."

I lean in to see the whole way is along the water. Sweet.

"Bread?" The waitress is back and she has put down a basket and is doling out little white plates.

"Could I have something else?" Kianna says, pushing the tall red drink towards the edge of the table.

If she's surprised she doesn't show it, just says, "Sure, what would you like?"

"A Fresca," Kia says looking right at her.

Uncle Luis must not have been sitting yet when we went through this last time because he doesn't seem like anything's wrong.

"She'll have a Coke," I say before the waitress can answer.

Kia pushes me and my sore side knocks into the wall. That hurts, but it was worth it to catch that waitress's smile at me.

"What's wrong?" Uncle Luis asks me and I realize my face must be screwed up from the pain.

"Nothin" I say, fixing it, putting on my liars face. *Second quarter second quarter second quarter.*

Kia reaches for the basket of bread and flips open the napkin it's wrapped up in to look inside. "What is all this?"

Uncle Luis leans forward to look. "It's a basket of mixed breads. That's rye and that dark one is pumpernickel, and this one looks like a sourdough roll." He picks up the roll up and sniffs it, then cracks it open. "Yep, it's sourdough all right." He reaches for the butter dish, opens one little packet and spreads it on the bread carefully in little strokes like he's performing surgery.

"You are seriously gonna eat something that's called sour dough. That don't make no sense you'd eat it knowing ahead it was sour," Kia says.

"It's good. Do you want a bite?" Uncle Luis holds out the unbitten half of the roll to her, but she turns away huffing. "Edgar, you want some bread?" he asks, pushes the basket my way.

I look in the thing but I don't see anything familiar so I just shake my head no.

Uncle Luis begins wiping breadcrumbs from his mouth corners with his napkin like this is some fancy place. "Let's get back to the map." He pulls the map back onto the middle of the table from where it's slid down in the booth beside him.

My side is still throbbing from when Kia pushed me. I make a move like I've got to get up and Kia moves out the way.

"Where are you going?" Uncle Luis asks.

"Bathroom," I mumble, and take off in that direction.

I see our waitress at the kitchen door talking to some guy in white. What is he like a cook or a dishwasher or something? She has a dark look on her face and she tilts her head so her red hair falls over her face. I feel for my chains.

She looks at me when I walk by. I give my head one nod the way I seen Mike do to the girls. I can hear his voice in my head saying *ladies* all smooth like. I don't say anything though, just go into the bathroom.

When I get in there and unzip my jacket I can see that it's leaked through onto my tee shirt and there's a nasty smell that's making a stain. This'll be the second wife beater I got to trash and it's only the second day.

I get a bunch of balled up paper towels, wet them and bring them into the stall with me. I don't care if they think I'm taking a dump, I can't risk Luis walking in again.

First I take off my jacket and hang it on the hook on the back of the door. Then I look down at the spot. Pulling up my shirt hurts like nut busting, but I do it slow and careful. When I put the wet towels on, at first it feels cool on the hot skin, but then I've got to hold back from howling. It kills. I take the wad off and stare at the wall.

"Take Rayanne," it says on the wall in black marker. Looks to be a Sharpie and I'm wishing for one right now so I could tag this bathroom.

"Edgar?" Uncle Luis is at the door. "Food's here."

I throw the wad in the toilet and flush.

"You feeling all right?" He asks nice, but I blow out of the stall like I'm going past him. "Hey, slow down, wash your hands," he says like somebody's mother, then disappears out the door.

In the mirror I see I'm just in my wife beater. I left my jacket hanging in the stall. Did he ask me if I was alright before he saw me or after? Did he see this mess on my shirt?

I get my jacket on quick and zip it up, then wash my hands. When I look back in the mirror I see my face looks red. I look kinda blotchy, ugly like. That's enough, I'm outa here.

Out the door and I nearly crash into the redhead walking with her hair in her face, holding a tray of dirty dishes.

"Watch it," she says as the dishes wobble.

"Sorry," I say, putting my hands out to steady the tray. This motion pulls at my side, but I don't stop.

"Oh, it's you," she says like I'm somebody she knows. "Your food's there."

"Yeah," I say.

"Your sister and your dad started already."

"Uh," I want to correct her but something stops me. "Thanks."

And she disappears down the hall. Finally I get to watch her go.

Chapter 13
Pennsylvania

The Liberty Bell is a letdown. I want to say that it's not all it's cracked up to be, but that would be too stupid a joke even for me. It's more like something Uncle Luis would say and I don't want to start sounding like him.

My stomach hurts from all that orange cheese in the Philly Steak. Edgar looked at me like he knew I shouldn't be eating it, but I went ahead anyway. Dairy products make my stomach hurt if I eat too much. Uncle Luis doesn't know this though, so he even bought me ice cream for dessert. Edgar almost said something then, but instead he just looked out the window. I don't think he's feeling too good either the way he didn't even eat much of his burger and then said nah to dessert. Edgar usually loves dessert.

Then he just sat outside on the steps and didn't even come see the stupid bell. He didn't even slump back like usual to look cool and ready for action. He just sat there kinda balled up. When I came running out to show him the spoon Uncle Luis bought me he looked all hot and bothered.

"Hey Edgar, look at this cool spoon with the Liberty Bell on the handle! It even has its own special case," I was telling him. I finally had the first real thing to go in my backpack, something I picked, something that was mine.

He looks up at me all slow and glassy-eyed.

"You alright?"

"Yeah," he mumbles.

"You look hot," Uncle Luis says, coming up behind me. "Why don't you take off your jacket?"

This seems to make Edgar mad, like Uncle Luis is suggesting he go naked. Usually Edgar likes to just wear his white shirts because it's not allowed in school and because he thinks he looks good in them or something.

He tries to stand up and wobbles.

"You all right?" Uncle Luis asks real nice.

"Why do you keep asking me that?" he say all mad. Then he gets up and we start walking to the car.

"It's time to get back on the road so we can make Baltimore by sundown," Uncle Luis says, changing the subject off Edgar.

The map he showed in the restaurant had the route in a nice peach marker and I pictured it in my head. "We go along the water for this next part, don't we?" I ask him, keeping the conversation going, holding onto my spoon in the case real tight.

"Most of it, once we get out of Philadelphia anyway." He is taking big breaths of the May air. It's real pretty, the way all the trees are opening up green and the way the houses are so neat and fixed up like.

I start doing what he's doing, breathing in the fresh air and it reminds me of that time with Miss Faith. People like spring air a lot I guess. I never thought on it too much but it's pretty good. I look to see if Edgar's breathing in the good air too, but his face just looks weird.

When we get back to the car though, Edgar reaches for the back door.

"You can't sit back there," Uncle Luis tells him.

Edgar ignores him and waits for the car to get unlocked.

"Really Edgar, there's too much glass still." Uncle Luis puts his keys in the driver door and reaches in and over to open the other locks. "We'll look for a car vac in Baltimore when we stop for dinner."

Edgar opens the back door and gets in.

Uncle Luis stands in the street watching him lie down. Then I see him take a big breath and let it out slow. I notice I'm doing it too. It actually helped my stomach feel better for a minute. Then we get in the front and drive off to the highway, leaving the cracked bell with Edgar lying on glass.

"What's that smell?" I ask.

"I see what you mean." Uncle Luis can smell it too.

"Edgar, you smell that?" I ask him, but when I look back I see his eyes are closed. He probably got high with that waitress while we were looking at the bell.

"What is it?" Uncle Luis asks, rolling down the window.

"Smells like something rotten," I guess.

"Is it coming from inside the car or out?" he asks me.

I try to sniff out the answer but it makes my stomach really hurt to try to smell that bad smell more. "I don't know. In, I think."

To take my mind off it I write in my diary:

Dear Diary,

We are just leaving the city of Filadelfia and Uncle Luis and me went 2 see the Liberty Bell. He bought me my first souveneer of my life and it's this perfect little silver spoon with a big bell on the end of the handle. It's in this plastic case that holds it in and makes a snap when you close it. I'm not gonna open it 2 many times tho because I seen its already starting to crack on the bend, like the top could break off the bottom in a hurry.

Like I said before I can't be just happy because even though I got my shiney spoon I also got a real bad stomack ake. I think it's the pain of not having Momi 2 see the big bell with Uncle Luis, but it could be the icecream. Or maybe it's the pain of bleeding. Maybe this is why some call it the curse.

Bye 4 now K

It's pretty soon after that when I threw up.

Something about how it was all curvy getting back to the highway and writing in my diary and the way Uncle Luis was doing that thing of stepping on the gas and then the brake. I think it was also the cheese and the ice cream, and then that weird smell in the car.

"Look under the seat, will you?" Uncle Luis asked.

I leaned over to look under the seat and my stomach lurched. "Hey Edgar, look under that seat will you?" I had to reach over and land him one to get him to do it. He jumped like I stabbed him.

"What the—" he started.

"Look under the seat while you're lying like that will ya?"

I didn't think he was going to but then I saw him reach under with his hanging hand. He felt around for a minute and then pulled out a nasty black bunch of plantains from Mrs. Perez.

That's when I puked.

Now we're riding along in the dark with the sky filling up with stars. I want to wake Edgar up to tell me their names, but he is totally out of it. When Uncle Luis made him get out at the car cleaning place he was so mad I thought he wasn't going to do it, but then he did. Usually getting stoned makes Edgar happy or quiet, but not mean.

Now everybody's happy though. Uncle Luis has a total clean car like how he likes it, Edgar gets to sleep on the back seat without getting cut up, and I have on clean clothes and a clean pad and my stomach feels way better. Only thing is, it's awful quiet with nobody saying anything, and I can't totally tell if they're not mad anymore.

Anyway that spray stuff Uncle Luis got smells like trees and the car looks way better than even before I puked so what's the big deal. I like riding with the windows down. It's just that Uncle Luis is all nervous and he keeps looking over at me and asking if I'm all right now. He's expecting I'm sick and I'm going to do it again.

"I'm not sick," I say.

"Good," Uncle Luis says back.

"No, I mean it wasn't sickness that made me throw up." Although I wonder if this bleeding made it worse.

"Oh?"

"No, I'm…well, I'm…."

"You're what?"

"Lactose intolerant," I tell him finally.

"You're lactose intolerant?" he asks like I didn't just say so.

"Yeah."

"How long have you been lactose intolerant?"

"As long as I've ever known," I say.

"You've known you were lactose intolerant? Always known it?"

"Well, yeah."

"You have always known it and you ate all that cheese and ice cream?" He's putting it together now.

I look out the window at the beautiful stars. "Yup."

If he's mad he doesn't say nothing, just drives. He's got his glasses all pushed up tight and his mouth is kinda pinched like he's got a splinter or something. Maybe he's wishing he wasn't on this drive, didn't have to take care of no one throwing up.

I saw him at the car place, when we had to wait for the inside to get cleaned, reading some book about loss. I thought it was about losing things like your keys until he closed it up when we were ready to go and I seen the second part of the title about children and grief. Uncle Luis doesn't have any children and so right off I knew there was something up about that. Then a few exits back it came to me that he was reading that book about me.

"What's that book say?" I ask before thinking.

"Book?" he asks.

I caught him off guard. Wonder what he's thinking on.

"What are you thinking about?" I ask.

"I'm thinking about what book you mean," he says.

"No, before I asked you that, what were you thinking about then?"

"Hmmm," he says all drawn out and I can't tell if he's stalling or if he really doesn't remember.

"Come on," I rush him.

"Your grandmother," he says then.

"Abuela?"

"Yes."

"What were you thinking about her?" I ask.

"About how she's going to look and if we're going to fight and all that," he says.

"Did the book say to answer all my questions honestly?"

"What book are we talking about now?"

"The one about children and loss or grief or whatever. The one you was reading in the car place."

"Oh," he says and that's all for a minute.

The sky is getting darker on this stretch of highway. I tilt my head back to see the sky.

"Yes, it says to answer all your questions honestly," he says in the quiet.

Without picking up my head I ask him real quiet, "How did Momi die?"

194 E G SLADE

I figure it's a hard one since no one told me yet, so I give him plenty of time by not looking over at him, just looking at all the millions and cajillions of stars up there. I see a patch Edgar told me the name of once. Something about a boy and his belt, Ryan maybe. I want to wake Edgar to tell me again, but then Uncle Luis will just think he's off the hook to tell me the truth.

"She was pretty far gone when they brought her in, and they just couldn't save her," he says real quiet like it's the funeral.

I can't help turning my head now. "Far gone with what? What was she sick with?" I don't mean to sound like that, but I have to know. The way I figure it they're not telling me because it's contagious and I must have it too from crawling into bed with Momi some nights since Popi's been gone. Either that or it's generic and I got it in my blood or however it gets passed down in families. Maybe Edgar's got it too. Maybe he's dying of it right now on the back seat and we're doing nothing.

At this I scared myself so bad I had to turn around and shake Edgar. "Wake up!"

Edgar moans. This scares the business out of me and I shake him again. "Eddie, wake up now!"

But still he doesn't wake up.

"He's gonna die of it!" I yell at Uncle Luis.

"What?"

"Edgar's dying! Do something." My voice sounds squeaky and babyish but I really feel freaked out by the way Edgar's acting.

Uncle Luis puts on his blinker and gradually moves into the scrubby area on the side of the road. He is doing it so slowly like it's not a total emergency. When he pulls over he leaves the car on and turns around to the back seat. The car place put in a temporary plexiglass thing in the back and sealed it in there, so there's light from the highway shining in on Edgar.

"Hey, Edgar," he tries.

No answer.

"Edgar," he reaches back and shakes his arm a little. Then he feels his forehead. "Jesus," he says soft. Then he looks up at me. "Sorry. It's just that he's burning up with a fever."

I reach back and feel his forehead and sure enough it is wicked hot. Then I get real scared. I start to cry on accident. Prayer that goes where I go runs across me.

"Hey, hey, it's just a fever. It's all right," Uncle Luis says like I'm small, but I'm glad he says it like that anyway.

"Let's find ourselves a hospital nearby with an emergency room and have him looked at," he says. And with that he puts his blinker on and moves slowly back into the highway traffic.

Uncle Luis is doing better at this than I expected.

Chapter 14
Maryland

He's burning up and not answering me, probably in a coma and if she vomits again that's it—I quit.

This was all I could think racing along down 95 towards Baltimore. I wanted to push the gas pedal down as hard as I could, and even though I tried every multiple including nines, which generally works on everything, it was this little line from the book running over and over in my head that kept me calm. *Patience, love and kindness, patience, love and kindness.* It didn't have anything to do with the situation at hand, but it kept me from breaking the law. Something about repeating it over and over was like a balm for my racing mind.

Now Kianna and I are waiting in the Emergency Room waiting area. They took Edgar back to a room after a big hassle over the insurance. They all wanted the paperwork filled out and Edgar was hanging on me, barely conscious.

"Here's my insurance card. We're from out of state."

"Where's his insurance card?" the receptionist asked, all pursed lips.

"He doesn't have one, he's on mine," I told her.

"Well, if he's on yours he should have his own card," she insists.

"Look, he loses things, all right? Just take mine." I push it to her and almost lose my balance.

I feel Kianna's hands steady me from behind.

The receptionist picks up the card and reads it. "Luis Santiago. And what is your son's name?" She puts her fingers at the ready on her keyboard.

"Edgar. Edgar Santiago." I hadn't thought about the benefits of having the same last name until just then.

"Address?" she asks.

I tell her my address, and as I do I feel Edgar lifting his head to look at me. I keep my eyes on the purse-lipped receptionist.

Then an orderly came out with a wheelchair and Edgar fell into it with a thud. I imagine they took him back there alone because they think he's on some drugs and he wouldn't say if his *father* was in the room. I don't know, I've been on a lot of drugs in my life and Edgar's condition just doesn't seem to add up.

Kianna is sucking her pinky finger like she does when she's worried.

"You want a snack?" I ask her.

"Like what?" she asks.

"Let's go see what they have in that machine down at the end of the hall there."

"What if they come to tell us about Edgar and we're not here?"

"Do you want to go alone?" I reach into my pocket for some bills to give her, but she shakes her head and looks real young. "You know, I think we'll be all right to just go down the hall a minute." But I can tell she's not budging unless I can do better than that.

I get up and cross over to the window. "We're here with Edgar Santiago and we're going to the vending machines for a minute, so if anyone's looking for us, that's where we'll be." Then I wave for Kianna to come and we go down the hall.

"You think he's gonna be alright?" she asks.

"Yes I do," I say more certainly than I feel, reaching down to pick up someone's discarded candy wrapper in the middle of the hallway. "He's young and strong and getting medical attention. So what'll it be?" I wave grandly at the machines like there is some great choice and deposit the wrapper in a nearby trash while she chooses.

Back in the green plastic chairs I realize I have fully lost track of time. That is not like me. I search the walls for a clock and then ask the woman with the ice pack on her head what time it is. How did it get to be eight forty-five? I guess it's dinner out of a vending machine tonight. I swore I was going to do better with the meal thing today.

Kianna opens her backpack and gets out her diary. She unlocks it and begins to write fast and furious. I realize I never answered her question about Callie's death. I guess what's true is that I'm just not ready to tell a ten-year-old that her mother died of a drug overdose. What sense could she possibly make of that? What sense can I make of that?

Staring at the way the chairs attach, I'm brought back to the morning going to identify Callie at Bay State. They made me wait in chairs identical to these, but in orange. I remember my hands were numb knowing what was coming.

∾

"Mr. Santiago?" A beautiful man in blue scrubs scans the room to see who will claim that identity.

I am slow, but Kianna stands and calls out to him, "Over here!" Her rainbow diary falls to the floor and the little key that's still attached clinks when it lands. She scrambles to pick it up, putting the cap on her gel pen.

I stand beside her as the man approaches. "Good evening. I am Dr. Finney. I've been with your son Edgar. Could you come back with me?"

We begin to follow him, but he stops. "Just you, Mr. Santiago. Your daughter will have to wait here."

I look down at Kianna. She shakes her head no. I nod my head yes. Her eyes fill with tears.

"I'll be right out. This won't take long. Right, Dr. Finney?" I look to him to back me up, but he is using the delay to make a note in the chart he's holding.

"Is my brother okay?" she asks Dr. Finney.

At this he looks up from his notes and smiles at her. "He's going to be just fine."

"Go on and have a seat. I'll be right back." The look on her face tells me this is almost more than she can handle, but she turns and sits back in the plastic chair she just left.

Back by the area where they have Edgar, Dr. Finney stops and turns to face me. He has close-cut black hair, a strong, jutting jaw, and a fetching five o'clock shadow.

"How well do you know your boy?" he asks, looking me dead on.

I know this game, so I return his look. "Very well."

"Did he tell you what happened with the knife?"

I don't have long to consider my answer to this without the delay being all the answer he needs. If I bluff him and lose I could be looking at a Department of Social Services call. If I tell him the truth I look like a liar for saying I know Edgar very well. I look for the answer in Dr. Finney's face.

"No," I say.

Dr. Finney exhales. That was the right answer.

"What happened with the knife?" I ask.

"He got cut in some kind of street fight, and it's brewing a bad infection. I guess the pain was getting to him, so he borrowed a painkiller from a friend and had a minor allergic reaction that put him out. He's better now. We have him on an IV drip of antibiotics. I'll give you a prescription for oral antibiotics for him to take for the next ten days. Make sure he takes all of it and doesn't stop when he's feeling better. When the IV is done you can take him." He's writing out the scrip while he's talking. Then he tears it off and holds it out to me. "Enjoy the rest of your vacation." And then an amazing smile and I am in love.

"Thank you—thank you for taking care of Edgar." I sound like a stammering idiot.

"Not a problem," he says, giving me a little salute and walking back to his post to get the chart for his next patient. I watch him go and am not surprised to find the back as pleasing as the front.

Then I push the curtain back to see Edgar lying on a gurney in a hospital gown. His eyes are closed, but I can tell he's awake.

"Hey," I say.

"Hey," he says back. His throat is gravely like he hasn't said much in a while.

"You want a drink or something?"

He opens his eyes at this and when he does I see he thought I was going to be mad. Maybe I should be mad. Maybe I should be real mad and slam my fist on the metal counter and say *what were you thinking mister*? But it would seem unnatural to call Edgar mister and anyway, I don't feel angry.

"You all right?" I say instead.

"Yeah." He looks embarrassed.

"You get sliced in the Big Apple?"

"Yeah," he says again.

"Why didn't you tell me?"

He tries to shrug, but it doesn't work out lying down so he says, "Dunno."

"You have to tell me this stuff…now that we're father and son," I joke.

He smiles then. "Yeah," he says.

"That worked out pretty good having the same last name."

"Where's Kianna?" he asks.

"The doctor made her stay in the waiting room."

"You think she's thinking about not having the same last name?"

This question surprises me more than Edgar hiding a cut from a knife fight. "Why do you ask?"

"Duuno. Just figured maybe it'd bring up the question."

"And if it does?" I ask.

Edgar is silent for a long time until I'm no longer sure he's thinking about it anymore, but then he answers real quiet. "She should know."

When he says it I know it's true and that I will be the one who will end up telling it to her, her story, the truth about who she is.

The curtain swishes open and for a moment I think I see Kianna's purple sweat suit, but then the curtain drops behind a wide-hipped black nurse with a potential mustache on her top lip.

"You're almost done here," she says, shaking the IV bag roughly. Then she crosses over to Edgar and I feel his fear of her and what she will do next.

I step forward. "What's your plan?"

"My plan?" she barks back at me.

"Yes, your plan. What do you plan to do now?"

"Are you kidding me?"

I want to say *yes, of course I am kidding you,* and run out to leave Edgar at her mercy. Instead I take another step forward. "I was just wondering if you could tell us what you'll be doing next so we can get out of your way here."

Unexpectedly she throws her head back and laughs a great puff of a laugh. "Aw honey, aren't you a funny one." And in one move she reaches down and yanks the IV out of Edgar's arm, catching the spot with a gauze pad and folding his arm to hold it in place. "Hold your arm up," she tells him.

Edgar looks stunned, but I imagine the worst is over now.

This parenting thing has you doing and saying things you'd never expect, being places you didn't plan on and then just going along with it like it was all perfectly normal.

The next thing we know the bug-eyed receptionist is back behind the curtain with us, waving papers at me going on about calling the insurance company and there being no record of any dependents. Now that I know Edgar is all right I can go back out and get the kids' MassHealth cards the social worker gave me. I have them in a manila folder with the other legal papers, like their birth certificates and the kinship custody papers from the courthouse that I'm supposed to deliver to Miami.

As the receptionist's glasses swing dangerously from the chain around her neck and her voice rises in pitch, Edgar and I accidently catch eyes, and a small smile comes between us.

Chapter 15
District of Columbia

Out the window a star catches my eye and for a time I let it relax me. Then I figure out it's some kinda city light and no star after all an I try to turn over.

I got the bed this time on account of being messed up from that pill the sexy waitress gave me. Seriously, that was bad. I would have made it fine fixing the cut up myself if it weren't for that pill she gave me. She was all mad when she found out I was younger than she thought I was and I even had lied and told her I was two years older than for real. How old she think I was—getting all bent about me being a fake sixteen?

It is pitch dark in here and my side is killing me or I'd get up and go look in the mirror right now. I want to see how old I could be. Eighteen maybe?

Better off lying here in the dark though because I probably look bad after not washing up all day. I'll do it up right before we leave here. Get back in the game.

It's so quiet in here that I can hear the spaces between the noises coming off the street. Dog bark, then big crashing quiet. Car passing, then another burst a quiet. I wonder if I'm still toasted from the pill or they gave me more in the emergency room. I did have a tube sending stuff into my arm. Maybe that's what's making the quiet so loud.

Right now in all the stillness what I feel is washed-out bad. My arm hurts where that tank of a nurse hauled the needle out like she was winding up for a corner shot at the pool table. I can just see her down the pool hall with all them ol men smoking their fat ones, waddling her way round the table looking for the best ball to knock into the corner pocket.

I used to go down there sometimes to fetch Juan for Momi. Watch him from the back for a while figuring what kinda person he really be. He seem so nice at times, then when he be hitting on Momi I think what kinda person is that? In the end I don't know what to think. He says he didn't do it, steal them guns. That some other guy gone and stuck them in his coat. But he's not saying what guy, so he's got to do the time.

See even in that there's something confusing, because you have to respect a guy who won't rat out his boys, or even those who aren't his boys. He'd rather go down himself than snitch.

Now Miss J, she made the whole thing—about ratting out—feel all messed up. This one time when Snarp started a fire in the bathroom and the ups had her sniffing out who done it, man I felt all messed up. She had me in her office saying all true stuff like how she knew it was out on the streets who set it and she knew I knew who it was and all that. I just sat there staring out the window to the pointy part on top a the church. I'm thinking there's no way I'm ratting out Snarp and he's not even one a the boys. Hangs out with TJ and them.

He's a total zero. Still the more she talks the more Miss J was making sense. I think that's why the ups put her on all the hard stuff. They can't find out a thing the way they come blasting in all hard and mean, ready to smack you down with suspensions. Word on the street is they don't care about anything but some numbers they have to keep in the district. I think they ought to get rid of all the higher-ups and leave the business to people like Miss J who's just trying to sort the mess out.

She told me the police was involved because it was arson and that they were fingerprinting and she didn't want anyone getting fingered who didn't do it. She told me this because she knew I was in there near the same time as Snarp and that the ups thought it was me what with all that was going down at home. They already threatened me and did all their moves and I just shut up and didn't say nothing. Then the Mister makes me sit out in the hall for like a year with all them little kids walking by, picking their noses, staring at me.

Anyway, in the end I told her it was Snarp and she was real cool about it, and it didn't come back at me for saying it. Not a lot a people watching my back like Miss J and I believe she was the best person to watch Snarp's back too. She sent me back to class and then waited until lunch to come by for Snarp.

She came in all casual like she was just saying yo, but then I seen her make her way to Snarp's table. Her walkie-talkie is buzzing, but she's not paying any mind, just breezing with the class. Before long, real smooth she's walking out the door with Snarp. He did thirty-day suspension for that.

So I ask myself, would I do the time for somebody else's messed up move? I don't know man. I'd like to say I would, but then when I think about how Miss J tells it, it sounds stupid. Like what if I were to have done Snarp's thirty days because I wouldn't say it was him? Then I never would've hooked up with Sonia and that would be some real sorry story.

And what if Juan had bailed out on the man who put those pieces in his jacket? Then we wouldn't be here in Washington, D.C. in a cheap hotel. Maybe even Momi would still be alive and none of that would have gone down. Not like I'm blaming him, but still. You miss it when you're stubborn like that.

Now the quiet is more than the sounds, these long stretches where I swear I can hear high-pitch buzzing which just ain't normal. I'm just about to say something just to hear a voice when Luis turns over in the other bed.

I cough to see if he'll say anything.

He turns his head back toward me, listening.

"Would you tell?" It just gets outa me before I know it.

He turns over to face me. "Would I tell what?"

I have to think clear how to ask this, and I'm not in my clearest thinking place with all the buzzing silence.

The clock on the table between the beds starts ticking loud now. Kia moves around under the blankets on the folded-out chair, then is still. It's real dark out, just the light from the cable box on top a the set.

"Edgar?"

"Yeah?"

"Would I tell what?" His voice is quiet and I feel like the dark is saying it's okay to talk.

"If you didn't do something someone said you did, and you knew who did it, would you tell?" I ask him.

Uncle Luis is quiet. He lies there probably thinking it over. Then I hear a rustling and after a minute I take a guess that he's fixing his blankets, lining them up right. I can hear a truck shooting by on the street and a car starting in a far parking lot. Makes me think a the time me and Jaquan tried out Mike's car at night in the parking lot of the Basketball Hall of Fame. Big Mike brought us down there and says "Go on, try it." Jaquan did it first, sitting all tall up behind the wheel laughing and pressing the gas and then the brake so hard we almost flipped through the front window. When I had at it I went so smooth that Mike kept whacking me on the back and calling me his second. "You gonna back me up at them parties this summer. Drive me home."

Only I won't be there this summer. I'll be in Miami, probably pushing a broom to make cash. What am I going to do not to go out of my mind down there?

"It depends," Uncle Luis says.

"On what?" I ask.

"Who's the person?"

"What person?"

"Who's the person who did the wrong thing?" And then I remember the question I asked him about snitching. "Is it somebody I care about or not?"

"Not," I say.

He rustles the blankets again.

"Yeah, I'd tell," he says.

"But that's ratting somebody out," I say.

"Edgar, have you ever heard of the word *karma*?"

"Not."

"It's from Eastern religions and it means what you put out will come back to you, maybe not right away but eventually. So what follows is the idea that we are each here to learn something through our actions.

"So?" What does this have to do with snitching?

"So I think if somebody messes up they should learn the lesson from it, not me. I make enough mistakes on my own that I have to learn from without having to learn from other people's mistakes."

"Then what does it matter if you care for the person or not?"

He's quiet again. Some car alarm goes off right out the front. Then a door slams and we hear someone cussing. After a minute the alarm stops. All the quiet is gone outa me now. I'm filled with noise.

"That's a good question. I guess for me, it's harder to watch people I care about learn things the hard way. Maybe if I can help them out by taking the rap now and then it'd be okay. Maybe too, if they watched me do the time for their crime it'd be almost as bad as doing it themselves. Then maybe they'd still end up learning the lesson. A total stranger would be different. He'd be laughing, thinking *sucker*."

From the way he says all this it sounds like he's been around more than I thought. I got a ton more questions flying around my head, but then Uncle Luis rolls over and faces the other way and says, "'Night, Edgar. You rest that side now."

Gibbous gibbous gibbous.

I can only lie on my back or my right side so I turn on my right side facing the lump of him. When I move I can feel the cut pull under the bandage. That geeked-out jack who cut me. I wish he was outside the door a this room right now so I could get him back for what he done.

Now right there I hear all the stupid meanness, all the stupid revenge. But still man, he cut me. He took his knife and cut me for no reason. That is messed up. And now I got a infection and have to take them horse pills three times a day all because a that.

I close my eyes and in my mind I can see the poster on the wall a the Planning Center, the earth with a peace sign through it. When I was first in there that time I beat out the first floor wall I didn't even know that forked thing was a peace sign. I thought it was a car thing you find on the front hood to a fancy car.

"You like my painting?" Miss J asked me.

I didn't say anything to her about it either way.

"A student of mine made it for me for International Peace Day."

"What's them lines through it?"

She looked at me to see if I was busting on her. Must have decided I wasn't, which I wasn't.

"It's a peace sign."

"A peace sign?"

"Yeah, a peace sign. Like this," she says holding up two fingers at me.

"Why do you care so much about peace?" This just came out and I didn't mean it to sound so strong. I kinda did want to know though.

"Hmmmm," she said, fixing that big print cloth wrapped around her cornrows. The Miss never let a question go unanswered and she always let you know somehow she was going to answer it, even if she didn't have the answer at the ready. "Why do I care so much about peace?" Repeating your question was another way she stalled on it. "I suppose because I think there is nothing more important."

"Get out," I told her.

"Uh-huh," she said, moving her neck like Miss Wilky.

I couldn't help a smile there.

"Whatcha gonna tell me is more important?" she says, going all street on me.

"More important than peace? Lots a sh—stuff."

"Like what?" Now she was asking like she really wanted to know.

"Money, a good house, car, yeah like a nice slick car." I was just getting started. Seemed like tons was more important than peace.

"And what if there was a war going on and all that was taken or blown up?" Her bushy eyebrows was raised.

"But there ain't no war going on in Springfield, Miss," I told her.

"That's not what I hear," she says.

Something about the way she was looking at me slowed me up from correcting her, got me thinking more about what she could mean.

"There are wars going on everywhere, Edgar. There are wars going on in this school even." She knocked a piece a something off her sleeve. "These are wars no amount of money or fancy cars are going to fix. They can only be fixed by people powerful enough to work for peace. People who'll take all their anger and instead of punishing the wall, put it into making things right. And when I say that, I don't just mean right for them, I mean right for everybody."

Miss J had that way of mixing things up so total that you couldn't hardly remember what you thought before you went in there. And sometimes it even took a little while before you remembered after you went out. But then the street is the street. You forget that, you get reminded the hard way.

Like the time I didn't take TJ down for looking all over my girl. What comes next is a total mess. But even then Miss J is sticking to what she says. I was all suffering and she starts talking about gratitude and being grateful.

I turn over on this springy mattress back towards the window and look out to see if I can see any real stars. There is so much city light that when I look real hard I can only see a few specks of stars far away. It comes into my head what I was hearing about galaxies. I got Sonia to read me one a them astronomy books Kia got from some book giveaway, and it had this whole part about galaxies and how there are these three different kinds. Let's see if I can remember what they are....

One a them is a spiral. I remember that because Sonia took her pencil from behind her ear and she drew one for me in the dirt. We were out back behind the South End Community Center after school one day. One a the first warm days and she drew one right in the dirt there. That's what kind we are in the Milky Way, like one a them pinwheels that spin in the wind with most a the stars at the middle and then more coming out like the arms on the pinwheel. Spiral galaxies are like this bluish color because there is all the gas needed to make new stars. We are in a galaxy, where new stars get born all the time. When Sonia read that to me I thought *I wanna be one a them new stars* but I didn't say anything out loud to her. I kissed her though. I leaned over when she stopped reading and I kissed her my gratitude. Maybe there's something to showing when you're thankful.

"Uncle Luis?" I whisper into the dark.

No sign a life from him, but I don't care. I say it anyway.

"Thanks."

The next morning Kia is gone.

I don't mean stepped out. I mean she is gone.

I think Uncle Luis might have a nerves breakdown on me about it too. He started out handling it, like it was just a routine thing her not being here when we wake up. But then he starts acting real weird and then he just starts to lose it.

"Where is she, Edgar? I mean it. Where did she go?"

I can tell from his voice that he doesn't expect an answer, like he'd talk to the furniture if I wasn't there.

"She should be back by now. Yesterday she was back by now," he says.

Then I remember she did go off after she hit me up for the money and came back a while later just fine. That's what he's thinking on, hoping for.

We'd both taken our showers and cleaned up, taking our time. I wasn't supposed to get the bandage wet, but hell if I was going to start another day smelling like the street. I just moved around careful to keep it as dry as I could. Then I quick changed it into a dry bandage from what that huge black nurse give me. When I come out, even after all that long time, still no Kia. Uncle Luis starts fussing, folding her blankets like maybe if he fixes them up he'll find her in there somewhere. Then he stops and I can tell he's seen something. I step in closer but I don't see it.

"What?" I ask.

He steps closer to the big push-out chair Kianna was sleeping on and points to the sheet he put on there for her. Then I see it, the spot of blood the size of a dime.

He looks at me all freaked. I am thinking hard on a explanation, but I can't come up with nothing.

"Did you lie here at all? Last night when we were getting set up? This morning when I was in the shower?" He's all desperate, but he knows that's not my blood.

I shake my head.

"Was your sister with you when the knife fight happened?" His eyes are lookin like Easter eggs.

"It wasn't no knife fight," I start to say, but then I change to just sayin the part he needs. "No, she wasn't anywhere near."

He snatches up the sheet and looks at it real close, moving his glasses down his nose to get a look. "It's blood, right?" He pushes it out to me.

I look at the sheet and see what I saw already when it was on the chair. A drop of blood. I nod my head.

"Oh dear," he says throwing it down.

Then he does something I didn't see coming, he grabs a book and locks himself in the john.

I stand there thinking it out, trying not to bend at all. Never knew standing up straight was such a job. Okay, so we're in Washington, D.C. just off the highway on some busy throughway named after a state. Kia doesn't know one single person in this whole city, does she? I think on that and decide she doesn't. Where would she go and why? What's the blood spot about? And what is Uncle Luis doing in the bathroom?

I go to the bathroom door. "Uh, I'm going out looking for her," I say.

He doesn't answer.

It kills to lean down to put on my sneakers, tucking the laces in without tying them, but I do it quick and leave.

The air outside feels fresh and warmer than I thought it'd be. The day is clear and the sun is already working. The fresh bandage I got on after the shower still feels tight, and I reach to hold that spot like everybody can see it. I stop at the edge a the busy throughway. The sign says New York Avenue I'm pretty sure.

Think: *If I were Kia, where would I go?*

"Hey!" It's Uncle Luis calling. "Get back here."

I turn and look at him in the doorway. I want to take off and just be free out here, but he looks so sorry and anyway I got no good idea about where to go here. My side throbs from getting my shoes on.

"Where you going?" he asks when I get back to the door.

"To look for her," I say.

"Where?"

I shrug and look away down the street at a Harley-Davidson roaring by.

"Wait, let's make a plan," he says.

Then I go back in and watch him spin in circles. He is really tripping on this. I don't know what else to do but take a load off and let him turn. Finally he winds himself up so tight he goes right out the door telling me to stay put. At least there's a television set.

Chapter 16
District of Columbia

The city booms in my ears; the screech of tires, distant wail of police siren, the steam hissing out of the drain covers. Bewildered, I start down New York Avenue feeling the sweat on my forehead and feeling immediately returned to my life here as a drunk and a drug addict. It is that out of control and I want it to stop. A rising panic grows in my chest and without realizing it my hand goes up to hold it.

There was blood on the sheet and now she is gone—swallowed up by the noisy, dangerous city and I don't have a single idea of where to find her. I am looking for the cold trail of a ten-year-old, lactose intolerant Hispanic girl, who is lost, who has left, who may be bleeding, who I am responsible for. I want to holler "Kianna!" in a boom that wakes oversleepers, stops traffic, stops this spinning in my chest.

I start at the square and count up. *81 90 99 108 117.* I try the cube *729 738 747 756*, but the rhythmic quality that usually helps instead feels like a lie. *Patience, love and kindness, patience, love and kindness*, I try, but nothing slows the run on-sentences that make little sense, are not organized, are not careful, are not thought out.

"Where's the nearest hospital?" I ask a man passing by, surprising us both.

"Is it an emergency?" he asks, looking at me clutching my chest.

It feels like an emergency, but then I don't even know how to describe the emergency. In truth, if Kianna has bled to death and died at a hospital, and I have to identify her body so soon after Callie….

The man must grow tired of waiting for me and decides it isn't because he points at the bus stop and says "Take the number 4."

Grateful for a plan, I walk to the plexiglass shelter to wait. To calm myself I'm studying the slopes of the architecture on the outside of a large church, when a bus pulls up. I get on, take a seat across from a bum sleeping with his head against the seat in front of him, and look out the dirty window. I have an urge to take out my handkerchief and give it a wipe when I see we are heading for my old neighborhood. The past is butting into the present. Though the man I am now would rather deny who I was then, something comes alive in me when I look out the window at the familiar sights.

I feel an odd looseness in my body, picturing myself walking this sidewalk as I was then. I was the most in my body I have ever been and at the same time the most disconnected. I filled it with anything that would numb the pain without asking any questions or thinking through to when it would wear off. My father's voice traveled in my head wherever I went, and only when I was the most incapacitated could I escape the shame and humiliation.

At the next stop a black woman with a head turban, nursing a baby, gets on and sits next to me so that I feel instantly squished. She's humming something spiritual and instead of feeling soothed I feel claustrophobic.

I look out the window again to get away, and at that moment we are passing the corner where my life changed.

It was a warm day, and I was in a tank top and tight pants crossing the street without looking when a hand grabbed my shoulder and pulled me back. A car screeched to a halt where I had been about to step, and the driver yelled out the window a long string of angry words in Spanish. I turned to look at the man who'd saved me and saw the image of my father—a man so close in appearance that if it weren't for the scar under his eye I might have believed it was really my father.

We stared at each other with my appreciation left stuck on my lips. He must have been appraising my red-rimmed bloodshot eyes, my gaunt face. Then, very quietly, he said, "This isn't your life, son. It's time to find your real life."

And I did. I left D.C. twenty-four hours later with everything I owned packed in an army-navy duffel and went to the Outer Banks to get clean. I'd heard from our landlord that there was work there with his cousin Carlos, and so I went to find out.

I have thought of that moment many, many times, but I have never been back to this corner. Is it coincidence that I am here now?

Suddenly I am filled with questions. What does all this mean? What am I doing?

What do I want? What is my real life?

I went into the bathroom this morning with one of those books and read a few sentences before I put it carefully down on the edge of the sink. I felt so frustrated I wanted to throw it, but the floor didn't look clean enough, and I would have had to pick it back up eventually.

The truth is, I am wearing down on being understanding and flexible and loving. I don't know that I can take it anymore, spending every minute trying to figure out what is going on with them. When I returned to Springfield I picked a life I want to have. One where everything is where I left it, where my routine is the same unless I change it, where patience is only something I need when they are out of coffee and making a new pot at the Third Street diner.

Out the window I see a man holding a little girl's hand. She is smiling and pointing at something in the sky. I look up to see what it is and find a pigeon circling. Just as the bus pulls away from the light I see the man laugh and wiggle the little girl's hand.

At the Liberty Bell there was one moment like that with Kianna. She said something about the crack that was so clever I laughed. What was it now? She was so surprised that I had laughed, surprised and happy, that she reached over and took my hand and we walked around like that for the next bit. People looked at us like we were father and daughter.

"Stop!" I unexpectedly stand and pull the cord over the window, surprising the baby so it stops nursing and makes a small cry.

"This ain't no stop," the bus driver yells back at me.

"I have to get off!" I shout at him, shuffling past the woman and her child into the aisle. He slows down some but doesn't stop, glancing up at me in the mirror.

"I'm going to be sick!" I yell.

The bum's eyes fly open, the brakes screech, and the bus pulls up at the curb. The back door opens and I get off, gasping for a breath, and for a moment it really is like I'm going to be sick. Dry heaves, and then I realize that I haven't eaten in a long time, since Philly when I had that Caesar salad, and now it is nearly a whole day later.

This thought brings on a dizzy spell. I sit on a bench and polish my glasses, hoping that will change something. When I put them on I see a prayer card on the bench beside me. I pick it up and stare at the face of Jesus. He has a cane in the crook of his arm and is holding a wooly lamb. His hand is petting the lamb's back, his head at a tilt. Jesus and the lamb have matching expressions, eyes down, faces serene, almost sad.

I turn the plastic card over and look on the back. It says: "The Lord is my Shepherd: I shall not want. In verdant pastures He gives me repose." I wonder if verdant is from *verde*, the Spanish word for green? That would make sense, green pastures. "Before restful waters he leads me: He refreshes my soul." That sounds good. I want to be led to some restful waters. I want my soul refreshed. I feel tears at the back of my throat, thinking suddenly of Callie, the day she lead me out of my father's house and brought me home to her family's apartment. The last time I saw my father, his words of hatred ringing in my ears, I had told him the truth about who I was, and that was so far from who he wanted me to be. Callie's hand was sure and steady, accepting me, taking me into her life as her gay brother.

"He guides me in right paths for His name's sake."

This card is a sign.

A small bird perches on the wrought iron fence. I look at its black back, the way its wings are tucked in like a monk's arms tucked in its robes.

That's it. I know where Kianna is.

Chapter 17
District of Columbia

I don't know exactly where I am, but I've been here since dawn. My feet are cold and my stomach feels raw, like it's been plowed. I don't really know what I'm waiting for, so I just sit.

It was very dark when I first came in the side door. The front doors were closed, but that didn't stop me. When I saw the spire I knew it was the only place to be and was determined to get in here. So when I pulled the side door and it opened, I slipped in and sat in this row.

It took a while for my eyes to adjust to how dim it is in here. I guess the glass on the stained-glass windows is so thick it's hard for the weak light to get it. Eventually though, the light broke through and now I can see the picture in the window is an outline of a man with his head tilted down with all blues around him. He's got a pointy nose and beard and he looks familiar. Up above I can make out the words "With malice toward none, with charity for all, with firmness in the right as God gives us to see the right."

I'm thinking on these words real hard, but not much is lining up to make sense except the "to see the right" part, which I'm thinking is like peer mediation, but I'm not altogether sure. As more light comes in I can see the little scenes on the side of the man in the middle and right away I know this whole thing is about Abraham Lincoln 'cause I seen his tall hat in one a them. It's like this window is telling his story to the people who come to pray here and hear the sermons.

I went a couple times to hear Father Brown's sermons. Not enough times to know what they call the stage with the red carpet up there, but I'll bet anything they don't call it the stage, like Father Brown is doing some show, though it is kinda like that. He makes his voice all big and thundery and then real quiet and slow. I don't understand none of what he's saying, but I like it, the stuff he used, like the pot of smoke he swirled around when he said all those words.

A door opens in the front and scares me to pieces, like I was that stained glass and parts of me were separated while still being together. I'm ducking down here real quiet. I think I sat for too long with my feet going cold because they're all tingly now and I don't like that feeling. I move some to get it to stop and this book falls out of a holder on the back of the pew in front of me and goes BAM. I stay real still. I can hear the shoes of the person coming down the aisle to me. My heart is having a fit. I make my fingers into fists.

The steps stop. I realize my eyes are crushed closed like when I was little and I'd hide by closing my eyes thinking if I can't see them, no one can see me. I open them. I see a black robe and black shoes. I look up the robe. The face up top is smiling.

I bounce to my feet. "Hi, sorry I was hiding. I got scared when you came in," I say. Miss Faith always said telling it right straight out was the best and it never hurt to do that with Father Brown. Besides what else was I going to do? Push him over and run away? Lie to a priest?

"Welcome, I am Reverend Ward." His whole round face is still smiling at me.

"Reverend? Aren't you supposed to be Father?" I ask.

He tilts his head to the side and looks at me like he's figuring me out. "In this sanctuary we say Reverend."

"Why do you say Reverend instead of Father?" I ask, feeling like it's something I got to understand.

This time he doesn't tilt his head, but nods it instead. "This is a Presbyterian church where we say Reverend."

I'm confused why they'd make it so complicated and call the Father Reverend so I figure it's got to mean something good. "What does it mean?" I ask him.

"Reverend?" he asks. When I nod he crosses his arms over his big chest in the black robe and nods his head again. "That is a good question. It means worthy of reverence."

I don't mean to sound stupid, but I just gotta ask him what's reference. I know Miss Theresa has a section in the school library about it, but we can't check those books out so I never looked there. "What's that?"

What I notice is that Reverends nod a lot more than Fathers 'cause he does it again and says, "Reverence is a respect for the sacred or divine."

I like that even though I keep asking him questions he doesn't quit on me or make it simple. Still I gotta think hard on the words he's using. "Sacred like a sanctuary!" pops out my mouth. At this the Reverend smiles his round face smile at me, and I think we're done with that, but all the sudden up jumps another question. "So what does Father mean?"

More nodding then. "In the religious sense, it means authoritative witness," and maybe he knows more questions will come outa this one so he adds "which is a way of saying that they are authorized, or allowed by the church, to witness and make official events such as marriages…."

It seems he's going to go on to try to explain that better, but then he changes over and asks, "But speaking of fathers, where is yours?"

I didn't see that coming so I move deeper into the row looking away from him. I don't have a good answer for him.

His robes swish as he moves in and sits down a little ways away. "I'm glad you came to this church, if you couldn't be with your father," he says, and then we sit quiet for a minute.

The light is strong enough to be bursting in the big Abraham Lincoln window and there's every color of blue filling up the room.

"And what about your mother?" comes his voice which he's made real soft now.

"She's dead," comes out.

That doesn't stop him for a minute though and it makes me like him. "I see," he says and even though

I'm not looking I can tell he's nodding again. "You must miss her very much." He says this like it's true and not a question.

Something about the colors from the amazing window and the kindness of him saying such a true thing to me makes my eyes sting.

He rustles in his robe, then hands me a white hanky. Don't know why this surprises me. Maybe I expected it to be black like his robe, or maybe I just never thought about a Father, or a Reverend, having a hanky up his sleeve.

I take it and let myself cry just a little.

We sit together for that part. Then he says, "Have you had anyone to talk to about your mother passing?"

"Miss Faith, at first, she's the school counselor, but then we had to leave and I won't see her no more, anymore." I want to talk the right way for him after he explained all that to me before.

"Did you have the chance to tell Miss Faith the story, or did she already know it?"

That's a real good question. Thinking on it, I guess she did already know and we talked about it like we both knew. "She knew, I think."

"So have you told anyone the story of your mother passing?"

"No, I guess I haven't yet."

"Would you like to tell me?" Maybe he sees my pause because he adds, "Many people come here when they need extra ears from God."

This is just the right thing to say, so I just start talking and telling him everything about living in Springfield and then Momi dying and us having to get moved to Miami. He asks about who "us" is and I tell him all about Edgar and the trouble with smoking drugs and not reading and then getting cut in a street fight and how he almost died in the hospital in Baltimore. He soon stops asking any questions and he just lets me say it all.

When I had it pretty much out he looks at me very kindly. "You may think you are talking only to me here, but you are being held by the loving arms of God. Wherever you go on your journey you will be held by the loving arms of God."

I think about what being in God's arms would look like. Maybe it's the window but right away I see God in a big tall black hat with a pointy black beard. I'm smiling at this when the Reverend throws me another curve ball.

"I notice, though, that you have not said much about your mother."

Then I remember the hospital and that smile falls right off my face, crashing onto the church floor. I remember how at that hospital in Baltimore I felt so alone in those chairs and how the next time those double doors opened I slipped through behind a man in green pants and top matching, and went until I heard Uncle Luis's voice talking with Edgar's doctor. I knew if he saw me, he'd make me leave because he already said don't come, so I hid behind this thing of laundry on wheels.

They were talking all on about Edgar and what happened and his medicine. That's how I know about the street fight. When the doctor left and Uncle Luis went behind the curtain to Edgar I was going to slip back there, but then a big black woman came to the counter by the laundry and I was afraid to move. I could hear them talking in there real easy though, so I just stayed crouched down and listened.

That's how I heard the thing that scared me. The thing so duh-of-course I can't believe I never thought of it before. My face falls into my hands thinking of it; Edgar and Luis have the same last name and I don't. Edgar knows why not, and he sounded like it was something to keep from me, and that made me real scared. I been thinking on it all night and then pretty soon after Edgar finally stopped bugging Uncle Luis and went to sleep I figured it out.

I got Popi's name, not Momi's. Edgar got Momi's name. The only reason I wouldn't get Momi's name is if she was not my real mother.

Chapter 18
District of Columbia

This is not for real. Sitting in this dump of a motel waitin' on what. At first I was all pissed off and pounding on the fake coffee table when the cable wouldn't work. But then I couldn't help noticing that it didn't change anything to get so fierce about something I couldn't fix. So then I lay out on the unmade bed in my clothes and took a nap. I thought about hitting the street for some weed, but I couldn't be sure what it'd do with them pills I got to take for my side. I figured it was enough trips to the hospital. Anyway, every time I been after drugs on this trip it's messed me up good. Better off staying awake, especially till Kia is back.

After I cribbed I went in to take a piss and I seen that book in the bathroom Uncle Luis has been so stuck on. It must be pretty good to keep carrying everywhere, so I brought it back into the room with me when I was done. There's a stuffed chair by the window that looks easy enough on my side, so I sit there and open the book.

The words are tough, but I'm making them out all right. *When there is loss.* Then something about children. It's some book about kids and geese. No it says grease. These words are all blurry. I just hold it closer, okay, now

I see that's a *f* at the end. It says grief. Kids and grief. Huh. He's reading a book about kids and grief.

The front page has all sections in it. I can't make out them all but there's one I see with a word I know: Anger. Page 59. I flip to it. Man there's a lot of words on this page with a big curly three for a chapter title. My stomach's growling and I'm all out for a snack. I'm about to throw the book down and go hunting for something, but then I picture Kia coming back to the room and thinking we was gone, just like when I went back to the gas station and they was gone. I don't want her feeling nothing like that.

My eyes skim over the page looking for words I know. It's mostly the small ones and I can't make no sense with just the small ones. So I go back through and look over the medium sized ones. The letters get all blurred and messed up, but if I wait a couple seconds my eyes can make them go straight. Still, I have to skip words now and then and so I can't get total what they're saying, but it's something about how being pissed off is a part of being sad. It said it's a "necessary" part, but I can't figure that word no matter how many times I go at it. I try it out loud but I sound too much like a retard. I almost throw the book at the cable box because they both are trying me today, but then I just decide to skip "necessary" all together. Who needs that big stupid word.

Words are funny how they make you feel. The Miss says I use curse words to defend myself, like weapons. I'd like to think that is bullshit, but then maybe saying that would just be proving her point. I'm going to try not saying curse words and see what it'd be like.

This book's getting on about how when someone dies you got to go ahead and be really ticked about it and find ways to blow off about it. Then something about power. Power-ful dis-tan-cer. What is a distanker? A powerful distanker is probably a really big one.

Anger is no problem for me anyway, so I go back to that page at the beginning and look for a different part. "Disbelief" is page 82. I turn to that and start skimming under the big curly five. I don't know what "disbelief" means yet. When I "chunk" it like Miss B said in remedial reading I get "dis" which I know what it means to dis someone. Then "be" which I know too. Like to be somebody. But the last part "lief" is messing with me. Something about l-i-e-f, lef. What is lef? Dis-be-lef. What in shit city is that? Man it's hard to stop cursing. Alright, what in sin city is that?

Then I remember something stupid, but great. I hear Miss B's voice saying "When two vowels go a-walking the first one does the talking." That means the "ie" says *eye*, so it's life! Dis-be-life! I fricking did it. I stuck with it like they always say and I figured it out on my own. This whole chapter is on disbelife, which must be something about not liking who you are in life and I know a whole lot about that. I should have written this fricking chapter.

Now I want to go on, but my stomach is killing me and I have to eat something. I set the book down on its belly marking the place and I scout out the window.

There must be a vending machine around here somewhere.

I go out the door and look around. Nothing but garbage blowing up against the building and then there's a tank for something. Well, if I don't go far I can see her coming and get back here.

Traffic is honking and the sun is high. It must be noon at least. I see a laundromat across the street and figure there must be a machine in there. I was wrong though, only soaps and junk in those machines. Down the block there's a liquor store, but when I go in there looking for peanuts and a Coke the man behind the counter yells at me, "Get outa here you underage spic." I want to curse, but then I see she'd be right about using it as a weapon so I just quit there.

I see a dog eating out of garbage can in the alley and instead of pity I feel rage. I hate that mongrel with its ribs all sticking out, looking all scared and dirty.

In the next block there is a store at last. I go in and it smells real strange. I don't recognize none of the foods there, but I'm too hungry to care. At the back they have a grill with some hot food. I look up at the menu for burger like always. It has messed up words like "hummus" and "tabouli" and some others just like that I can't make out at all. The strangeness has worn off and now it just smells like food cooking and I want some.

"I'll have the special," I say to the dark man in the white apron.

"Couscous or tabouli?" he asks.

"Either one," I say shrugging like I like them both.

"How about some of each? A young man like you needs a big meal to fill him up," he says with a smile.

"Thanks," I mumble.

At the counter a woman wrapped up in some kinda robe thing takes my money. She smiles when she gives me the change and I think, maybe my luck is changing right here.

Out the store I practically run back to the motel looking for Kia the whole way. For a minute I see a girl in a pink sweatshirt and pants like hers with dark frizzy hair, but when she turns her head I see it isn't Kia at all. In fact it's a woman who's kinda old even, and black, and I feel a little freaked out.

I go in the room and pull my food out the bag and on the top of the container the man has wrapped up a whole big piece a this real flat-looking bread. I tear into it like I haven't eaten in days. It does kinda feel like that. I pop open the top and I begin shoveling the food from the different sections of the Styrofoam container into my big empty self. I hardly taste it, but for one section that makes my tongue burn. Sh—crap, I forgot a drink.

The clock radio goes off and scares the crap outa me. It's some kinda music with no words, like a piano and something else. I go over to shut the thing off when that other instrument comes in real quiet and gets bigger, like a feeling for a girl. Like Sonia. I sit on the edge of the bed and miss her. Her light face and her strong chin, like she could take it, but then her real soft eyes, like maybe she couldn't. I don't think I understand girls too good. They never do what I think they're going to. Like I never would have expected Kia to be gone this morning for so long. Maybe someone else would've seen that one coming, but not me. Makes me think a little nicer about Juan for all he tried to figure out Momi. She wasn't easy to understand.

This music is making me sad, thinking about all these girls who are gone to me right now. I hate to be sad. It's dangerous.

I snap off the clock radio. Who sets the alarm for the afternoon anyway? That's messed up.

Back at the table I finish the food from their separate sections. I used to have a Big Bird plate with sections like this. I loved how it kept the food from touching and it made these little walls for pushing the food against. The day Momi let Kia use it I threw it up against the wall and broke it. I remember she didn't say nothing about it, just walked out the room taking Kia with her, and let me clean it up. There was some gross baby food she had put in there rolling down the walls like diarrhea and I just stood there for a long time staring at it thinking about nothing. Then I hear Juan's feet on the stairs coming up and I get to cleaning it up before he comes in and sees it. He was at his worst at the end a the day when he got off shift at Smith & Wesson.

Nobody said nothing about that plate after that, but I missed it something serious for a long time. My food was all in each other's face and I spent a lot of time worrying after that with my fork and spoon. Makes me want to wash the container out and keep it. How messed up is that?

With that music come on and now off, the room seems quieter than before, even though I can still hear the traffic and the street. Where is Kia at and how long is Luis going to keep me hanging here?

I go to the window and watch a scrawny old cat pick its way across the brown grass in front a this place. Its ears have tufts of hair sticking up off them and it walks with a limp. I take my tray out to the front.

"Here kitty," I call.

It stops and looks at me like I am dirt.

I ignore its attitude and kneel down with the food. "Want some?" I ask it real gentle.

It's staring. I see a piece missing from one a the ears and I decide it must be a he.

"Come here boy," I call.

Real slow and casual like, he walks over closer, then rubs against the side of the can someone set out there for cigarette butts. Must be to keep people from smoking in the rooms.

I set the tray down and back up into the room. Then I sit down on the puke colored carpet and wait. I got nothing better to do than wait.

Chapter 19
District of Columbia

Finally I had something better to do than wait. I had an idea.

The Presbyterian church on the corner of New York Avenue is just a block or so from the motel. I knew even before I pulled open the heavy door that Kianna would be in there, and sure enough she was, sitting in one of the pews on the side talking to the priest. Even though I was so confident, I just about cried when I saw her there.

I have stood back here catching my breath and getting myself together since I walked in a few minutes ago. It has taken a minute for my mind to focus on where I am, but now I can see what a beautiful church this is on the inside. Discreet and tasteful, the floors are polished wood and the altar is raised, but still in a lovely light wood. Behind there is a spectacular organ with dark wood at the base and silver pipes rising to the tall ceiling. In the center section is an ornate cross.

I reach into my pocket and feel for the Good Shepherd card. "The Lord is my Shepherd: I shall not want." But I do want. I want so many things. Mostly though, I want Kianna to be safe and she is. Maybe that's what

236 E G SLADE

it means, that if I have faith then the most important wants will be met.

As I walk up to the pew where Kianna is sitting I notice the second pew on the opposite side is a dark mahogany, whereas the others are painted white with light wooden trim. My shoes are noisy, and the two of them watch me come. I want to point and ask why that one is out of place. Why in a sanctuary so meticulously cared for is there such an obvious mismatch?

"You must be Kianna's uncle," the priest says confidently. "Welcome to the New York Avenue Presbyterian Church." He gets up as he says this and leaves his spot on the pew. "I have many things I must tend to before services this afternoon. Sadly, one of ours has passed and we will be gathering to remember her. I was saddened to hear of your recent loss as well." At this point he is beside me and he puts his hand on my arm when he says it.

"Thank you," I say. "We haven't gotten used to it yet."

"Of course not. These things take time." And he looks right into me with a look that can only be described as loving. Then he turns back to Kianna. "Remember our talk, God's arms," and with a small gesture of his hand he is gone, his robes swinging around him.

I'm afraid to look at Kianna, afraid of what I will find in her face, but when I do there is softness there. I move in and sit where the priest was, or is it a Reverend here? I am scattered by all the thoughts and feelings that continue to come at me, so I close my eyes and take a cleansing breath. What better place to get re-centered than a church?

I breathe in and out evenly, counting to five on the in breath and five on the out breath.

"I need to tell you some things," I say, opening my eyes and looking at her.

"Okay," she says steadily.

"I was the son of a very prominent banker in Springfield."

"Momi's father was a banker?" she asks.

"Let me finish," I say. "Let me get the whole thing out while I can, and then you can ask whatever you like.

"Okay."

"I was the son of a wealthy family in Springfield. When I was in middle school, about Edgar's age actually, I realized that I loved boys and not girls. My father was very angry about this and told me to leave his house and never come back. Your mother was my best friend and she was with me when this happened, so I went to her house. I ended up never leaving. Your grandmother took me in, fed me, and gave me a place to live. By the end of the year I had become a Santiago. Don't get me wrong, she didn't accept "my condition," as she called it, and spent many nights praying I would be saved, but still she took me in." I look at her to see if she understands what I'm saying. I can't tell, so I say it very clearly: "Your mother wasn't my sister by blood."

"So you're not my real uncle then?" Her voice sounds scared.

"Yes, I'm your real uncle. I grew up as a brother to Callie, your mother, and that makes me your uncle."

She doesn't look ready for this, but it is time anyway. "The reason I'm telling you this is that if I've learned anything it's that blood doesn't make us who we are. It doesn't control who we are to each other."

"So we don't have any of the same blood?"

"No," I say and take a breath before the hard part. "And you don't have any of the same blood as Edgar either." I feel dizzy when I say this, but to my surprise Kianna is calm and takes this news as if it were expected.

"Tell me the story," she says, looking at her hands.

I look over at that odd pew that doesn't match the rest but is still part of this place, and I begin talking. "Callie and Edgar were living on Union Street, and she was working at the 7-Eleven. You had just been born, but your mother had died and Juan kept coming into the store for things. Callie fell in love with you, took you both in, and the rest is history." I don't mean this to sound so pat, so buttoned up. I touch her hands. "She loved you as much as any mother ever loved her child. That's real."

I don't know she is crying until a tear drips onto my hand holding hers. I reach my arm around her and hold her. She comes easily to me and lets her tears fall.

The light of the day is now in full strength through the windows and the room is glowing. The organ pipes are glistening. The cross is strong. Kianna and I sit there until she is done.

"I have something for your backpack," I say. She wipes her face on her sleeve and looks up at me. I take the Good Shepherd blessing card out of my pocket and hand it to her. "I know it's probably not the same as the one Mrs. Perez gave you, but—"

"No, it is," she says, looking at me all surprised. "Where did you find it?"

"I guess you could say it found me."

She hugs me with both arms. "Thanks Uncle Luis."

And I know she means in a bigger way than just about the card.

"Where's Edgar?" she asks, slipping the card in her sweat suit pocket.

"Back at the place. You ready?"

"Yeah, I'm ready."

"I'm glad," I say, not trying to be meaningful, but then it is and it is the truth. Strange how after you sit quiet in a sanctuary like this everything you say seems more important somehow.

Her stomach growls. I take her by the hand, and we leave the church heading back to the motel.

ʊ|ʊ

It's a pretty big surprise to walk into the room and find Edgar reading a book with a cat on his lap.

"His name is Phantom," he tells us, putting the book down.

I see it is my book on loss. Is this for real? Edgar reading a book about children and grief?

Kianna rushes over to pet the scrawny thing. "Oh, he's so cute. Can we keep him?"

"Where did he come from?" I ask.

"The street," Edgar says.

"He needs food," Kianna says.

"I gave him the end a my lunch a while ago."

"Speaking of food, is anyone hungry?" I ask them.

I say this to avoid answering the question about the cat, but I can see they both must be starving because they instantly begin throwing things in their bags to get out of here and get a decent meal.

I look over at Edgar and see he is using both his arms again. His side must be healing. I don't want to embarrass him, so I wait until Kianna is in the bathroom. "Did you take your medicine?"

"Twice today already," he says.

"With food?"

"The second time. First time I didn't have nothing."

"Sorry about that," I say.

"Nah, it was nothing." And then he looks directly at me. "You had to find Kia, right?"

Right there, in that moment, something passes between us, like I am the head of the pack now. I was out doing what the head of the pack would do.

"Right," I answer, and then it is done, settled.

When I pick up the book about loss to put in my bag I see the rolled-up sheet from Kianna's chair bed, and for the first time all day I remember the blood. Just then she comes out of the bathroom, and instead of shying away from it, I just go to it.

"Did you get hurt yesterday?" I ask her.

"What do you mean?" she says, stuffing her toothbrush into her suitcase.

"There was blood on the sheet," I say.

Her face is still, blank, but with a thousand words rushing beneath that. She glances at Edgar, who is pretending not to listen, then back at me.

"Whatever it is, you can tell me," I say like I'm talking a jumper down off the Civic Center roof.

"My bloods started a couple days ago," she says, her face still blank.

At first I can't make out what she means. Maybe it's the hunger, but my mind is slow. Then when I do figure it, I am surprised. Partly surprised it's so early for her. She's only ten. And partly surprised that I don't feel at all uncomfortable. It is just a new fact about her.

"Oh." I wait for the right thing to say next. "Do you need anything?"

"Nah, I got it already. Back in Jersey."

"New Jersey?" Edgar says.

"Yeah, thanks for the fiver. I owe you." She picks up a pillow and hits Edgar with it once and then twice.

"What's this? Payback?" He grabs a pillow off of the bed and heads for her.

They are laughing. I am amazed. This day is full of surprises.

Chapter 20

Virginia

I think this day is gonna be full a surprises. The morning is so nice and my hair came out real good. Edgar let me have the front and Uncle Luis is doing his humming. How can I be so happy when yesterday I was so bad off, sneaking out feeling like it was the worst day ever. Now here I am in the front seat matching it in my favorite red tee shirt with the puffy sleeves, my hair looking so good.

I guess it don't have to make sense to be true. Like all that stuff Uncle Luis told me in the church and then we went and told Edgar at the restaurant. Uncle Luis did mosta the talking, about us not being his actual niece and nephew on account a Momi not being his real sister and not my birth mother neither. It seems like Edgar already knew about the Momi not being mine part. At first I was a little upset that he knew all along and never told me, but that lasted all of thirty seconds and then I gave it up. But he was real surprised about the Uncle Luis part. He was asking more questions than I ever heard him ask before, and I mean ever. He asked all about Uncle Luis's real father and if he knew him now and how it came to be that he got the Santiago name and all kinds a stuff. He seemed to take it pretty hard that they didn't have any of the same blood, and I was thinking the whole time that none of us have the same blood. And maybe they were too, because then we just sat there over the plates in quiet like we were strangers.

Then we drove for a while and let the road fill the space. I wrote in my diary.

Dear Diary,

Now we left Washington dc without meeting the president or even seeing anything just the inside a nice church witch was a good place to see cause there was a president there. I even saw his real true hat in a case on the way out the church that said he went there to pray like me.

Wish I had someone to tell that to besides you. I seen two things a history on this trip now—the bell and Lincolns hat. I'm practicaly famos.

But now nothings like I thought it was. Luis isn't my uncle and Edgar's not my brother. They both just people I ended up with. Momi held us all together and she's dead.

Bye 4 now, K

p.s. The blood is almost done now witch is a good thing because I'm about out of pads.

I learned a lot yesterday I didn't know. After that I had a bunch a questions coming to mind, like what about Popi? I asked Uncle Luis when we were in bed with the lights out last night if Popi gave me up. He was quiet for a good long time but then he said yeah, he had to because of being incinerated. I guess you can't keep no kids when you're in jail. But then I asked wasn't he gonna get out and Luis said not soon enough, he had to wave at his rights to being a parent and the court gave me to Abuela.

The place we slept was outside of Richmond in some place called Jarratt. Now I keep seeing signs for this Virginia Beach and I already bugged Uncle Luis for a detour, but he keeps saying he's got a better plan.

"Hey Kianna, get out your notebook," Uncle Luis tells me. I reach around in my backpack until I find it and one a my pens.

"Okay, I got it," I tell him.

"Find the page with the bumper sticker list. I see a good one."

Before I flip through the pages I look to see what he sees, and there it is on the shiny bumper of a long silver car. I read it out loud, "*No God in the classroom. Hell in the hallways.* What does that mean?"

Uncle Luis is chuckling. "It means the driver thinks there should be prayer in school."

"Prayer in school?" Edgar echoes from the back, where he holds Phantom asleep on his lap.

I get to the right page and write it down while it's still in sight.

"Look, there's another," Edgar says, leaning forward.

"In case of rapture this truck will be unmanned," Uncle Luis reads.

"What's rapture? Like a velociraptor? Like some kinda bird?" I'm guessing wildly.

Uncle Luis is laughing again and even though I don't see what's funny I understand his good mood.

"Rapture means to be transported by emotion…." He stops and then starts again. "It means to be really, really happy. It also means to be taken to heaven. How do you know about velociraptors?"

"Timeline of Life," Edgar and I say at the exact same moment.

Now it's time for Uncle Luis to be confused, but I'm too busy writing down the rapture one to explain and Edgar is looking out the window again. "What was the end? In case of rapture this truck will be…what? Empty?"

There is silence while they both think.

"Speed up," Edgar says, spying the green truck it was on up ahead a few cars.

Uncle Luis presses on the gas and puts his blinker on to get in the passing lane. His face is all concentrating and I giggle a little watching him. He hears me and exaggerates it even more gripping the wheel and sticking his neck forward with his tongue out up over his top lip. Then I really laugh.

We stopped at another rest stop and got snacks. Uncle Luis is feeding us a lot today, but I say get it while you can, so when he says pick anything I choose kettle corn and orange soda.

I went into the bathroom while he paid and my blood seems to be over. It was heavy like I was bleeding to death and then it practically stopped total. Now there's nothing. I thought people said you had your period for years, but mine didn't even last a week. So that's it I guess. I had my period. Now I can have a baby someday. I don't know what all the fuss is about really, if that's it. It wasn't so bad. Now I can throw away the rest of these Kotex. They must make them in these big packs in case you're the kinda person who has it for years. I'm real glad that's not me. I was barely ready to have it for the few days I had it, let alone years.

When I told Uncle Luis and Edgar about getting it back when we were in D.C. I thought Edgar might die of embarrassment. He started a whole pillow fight to get off the subject, but that was real fun so I didn't care. Plus now maybe he won't make me pay him back the money I borrowed because he won't want to bring it up.

Uncle Luis didn't seem anything about it. I mean at first he was all on about the blood on the sheet, but after I told him he was all normal about it like I said I had a bloody nose but now it's fine. Maybe he doesn't think it's a big deal because he's a man, and maybe it's not a big deal really, but I feel different. I feel more breakable, like I could get hurt more easy now or something. That is so stupid. But for real I felt like that a few months ago when we were playing kickball for outdoor recess in the parking lot, and I took one in the chest. The ball flew off Jerome's foot and socked me right in the chest. It probably would have hurt anyway, but it was the first time I noticed feeling on my chest, like sore spots there. I had the same idea that day, that I was more breakable than I used to be. Like I was something fragile now I had to protect from getting hurt.

I miss being able to do whatever I want.

Someone should have warned me.

But then Xoshell and Ramona and them, it seem like they like it. They never play kickball anyway, just leaning up against the fence, protecting their nails, jabbering on about stupid stuff. If having had my period makes me like that, talking about stupid stuff then I want to give it back. I can wait to have babies. Me and Tenise already pinky swore on that after her sister got pregnant and had to drop out of eighth grade. She was a class ahead of Edgar, but I asked him anyway if he knew who knocked her up. He just shook his head and went on eating his cereal.

Tenise told me her sister cried real bad when the baby was coming out. She had the baby down at the Holyoke Hospital with the midwives so Tenise got to be in there the whole time. I made her tell me the complete story without leaving out a single thing and it took her a lot of time to tell me everything. She said the midwives were real nice and they spoke Spanish even though they were white, or at least the two Tenise saw were white anyway. They let her help at the beginning, giving her stuff to do so her Momi wouldn't get mad and swat her like she does. But then things got real bad and Tenise's sister was yelling and saying curse words and trying to get up to leave. She told everybody she couldn't do it and she was leaving. Tenise said that part was scary but I think it sounds real funny, the picture of a big pregnant girl about to pop out a baby trying to leave in her little gown all untied in the back.

The baby came out a girl and I guess Tenise's mother cried about it. I said "Why'd she cry about that?"

And Tenise said, "She say she's too young to be a grandmother."

"That's why she was crying?"

"And because the baby was a girl," Tenise said.

"What's wrong with the baby being a girl?" I asked.

Tenise shrugged and picked at the gum on the back of the seat. Then she say, "Because she say girls bring trouble."

"What kinda trouble do girls bring?"

Tenise looked at me real blank-faced. "Babies," she say.

"Entering North Carolina," Uncle Luis reads off the highway sign. "Look at that map for me will you Ki-anna?"

I take up the map from above the visor where he tucked it this morning when we got on the road. "What do you want to know?" I ask.

"How far to Rocky Mount?" he asks. "Remember how I showed you to look in the legend down in the corner to calculate the mileage."

On the MapQuest sheet I seen they put the miles on there. I pick it up to look, but it only says the miles from Richmond. I see it says Rocky Mount is where we get on I-95 and then that's the last direction till we get to Miami.

"Looks like it's direct from Rocky Mount to Miami," I say.

Uncle Luis nods, but doesn't say yes or no.

It feels like the trip is about to change.

"Use the map, Kianna," Uncle Luis tells me.

I fold the map over and use my fingers to calculate. My tallest finger is sixty miles. I've never before had anything useful to do with my middle finger. This is gonna be fun. I hold up my middle finger and show him.

"This is sixty miles!"

He glances over at me, "Very funny Miss," he says with a half-smile. "Measure on the page, will you?"

From where we are to Rocky Mount is about half my middle finger. "I'll guess thirty miles," I say.

"Thirty miles. Great." He smiles, and I think that's all the math for now, but then he comes up with a good one. "If we're traveling sixty miles per hour, how long will it take us to get there?"

My finger won't help me with this one. "How do I figure that out?"

"Thirty minutes," Edgar says from the back.

"That's right," Uncle Luis says.

I turn around to see Phantom on his lap batting at a piece of thread Edgar must have pulled off something and is dangling in front of him.

"How'd you get that?"

"Don't know," he says. "The number just came into my head."

I turn back around to Uncle Luis, "What's in Rocky Mount?"

"With any luck there'll be a laundromat," he says.

I was awful careful to roll up my soiled underpants and stick it deep in my suitcase, but still I feel it's better to change the subject. "Have you ever been there before?"

It was just a question to get him off the trail but to my surprise he perks up. "Yes, how did you know?"

"Just a guess," I say. "When were you there?"

"Just after you were born I came south for a few months to get away from winter."

"I remember that," Edgar says.

"You do?" Uncle Luis is startled by this.

"Yeah, you brought me back that fish."

Uncle Luis is shaking his head. Phantom lets out a little meow.

"Can I hold her for a while?" I ask.

"Okay," Edgar says holding the cat over the seat. "It's a him."

I take him into my lap and stroke his slate gray fur. His ear has had a problem and is partway gone. It's all jagged on the edge like the side of a fancy Valentine. He's all tired out from playing with Edgar and he just curls up small and tucks his head under his tail. I don't mind though. We never had a pet before and I just like having him there.

I didn't think Uncle Luis was going to agree to have him after the night he gave us with his sitting on each of our heads and yowling till Edgar let him out. Edgar must have gone out with him though because awhile later I hear the door again and he came back in.

"Is he gone?" I asked from my sleep.

"Nah, he's here," Edgar said real quiet putting the cat in my arms.

But the next morning Uncle Luis didn't say nothing about the night. We all just showered and packed to go and along comes Phantom like he's part of the family.

"How'd you get him to come back last night?" I ask Edgar now.

"He never left," he says.

"What were you doing out there then?"

"Watching the stars," he says.

"What did you see up there?" Uncle Luis asks.

"A lot," Edgar says.

"Like what?" Uncle Luis says this like he for sure wants to know, not like it's a quiz or anything.

"The dippers and the Pleiades," Edgar tells him.

"How many in the Pleiades again?" Uncle Luis asks.

"Seven,"

"Could you see all seven of them?"

"Yup."

"What do they look like?" I ask, feeling a little left out not being able to picture what they are talking about.

"They're pretty close together," Edgar says. He's not so good at describing stuff.

"It's a small cluster of stars that catch your eye because they are so close in such a big sky." Uncle Luis adds.

"I want to see them," I say.

"Maybe tonight," Uncle Luis says like he knows a secret.

"Where will we be tonight?" I ask.

He hesitates.

"Where?" I am even more interested. "Where will we be?"

Then he gives in, "On the beach."

Edgar leans forward. "The beach?"

"Okay, yes. I thought we'd get our clothes washed up and then take a little detour to a place I spent a lot of time."

"Rocky Mount?" I guess.

"Nope."

"Is it in North Carolina?" I ask.

"Yes," Uncle Luis says. "It's a beach on the Outer Banks. It's part of a national wildlife refuge."

"What is that?" I ask.

"A protected place."

That sounds good to me. I could use some time in a protected place. I feel myself getting excited now, like this could be like a vacation.

I look back at Edgar and see his relaxed face. Not the stoned one, but the one I used to know. My brother is happy.

My brother is happy, my uncle is making his humming noise, there is a cat sleeping in my lap, and we are going to the beach.

Chapter 21
North Carolina

We are going to the beach. I keep thinkin a this between pages of my book. I never took to a book before. Just never found one that I had to know what it said enough to read it. I didn't think that book was made till a hour ago after we stopped in Rocky Mount to wash our clothes and get some stuff for our trip out to the beach. Seems Uncle Luis spent some a his money in the bookstore and he found me a book on stars like none I ever held before. The pictures are in color and the words are just the right size for my eyes. And it's a new book, not old and beat up like the ones I seen before. This is like all the real modern science about the stars, like stuff people just figured out. I'm holding it like I never held a book before, like how I used to hold Sonia's face in my hands. I wish I could show her this book. She'd be real impressed and real happy for me too that I got such a fine book and am going to the beach for the first time, all on the same day.

Kia got some chapter book she hasn't taken her nose out of neither. Something religious I think because it had God in the title. I read the first few words easy, something like Are you there God? Anyway Luis just got in the car, reached in his bag and tossed them to us saying "You can't go to the beach without a good book."

Now I have to take a break from looking in the book and look out the window because what is out there is incredible. I can't believe how big the sky looks over the ocean and if I ever seen the ocean before now I sure don't remember it like this.

"Kianna, come on out of that book and look around," Uncle Luis tells her. "There will be plenty of time for reading when we get there."

She ignores him for a minute, but when she does look up the book goes down. "Wow!" she says. And then that's it, because there really isn't anything more you can say about seeing it like this.

"What is this place?" she asks after we be staring and staring for a good long time.

"This is the Outer Banks," Uncle Luis says. "If you look on the map you can see that it is a long thin piece of land just off the coast of North Carolina."

Kia rustles the map, finds where we are real easy and then points it out to me.

It's so small it looks blurry. I hold the thing closer. She shows me again.

"There's water on both sides a us?" I ask.

"That's right," Uncle Luis says.

I try to pretend I'm looking down at us from the stars, seeing our car rolling along on this skinny piece of earth between water. But I can't picture it. Instead I picture my napkin on the blue table at the diner where we ate after we left D.C. with Phantom. Uncle Luis cleared his throat and I knew something big was coming. Sure enough he started talking all about the past and telling me something he told Kia when he found her in the church, bout how he's not for real related to Momi, how he's her adopted brother, just like how me and Kia is not real blood-related. I was surprised then that he was talking about it so open like that and I looked to see how Kia was taking it. When I did I saw she was looking at me for the same reason, and our eyes met. I haven't looked at my sister real direct in a long time and I thought she looked more grown since the last time I did.

She wasn't looking away so I didn't either and then I think we were talking without words like we used to. I was saying "It's okay," and she was saying "That's right." Then I said something to her I couldn't figure in words but she said back "I'll never leave you either," and that helped me get what I was saying to her.

Ever since that meal, things have felt easy and gone better, like we all worked something out. I don't know what it was for Luis but it was something because he's acting different too. Like he's thinking about things different now.

I'm not sure what I think about what he said, not being the real brother, but the way he said it with the other part, about me not being Kia's real brother neither, kinda makes it feel like less a big deal. Like so what. Then I figure out real slow why he's got to dump us in Miami.

Now we're pulling into a parking lot and I see something that makes me want to yell out, but I just hold my seat.

"Edgar, did you take your pill at lunch?" Uncle Luis asks.

"Sh—shoot," I say digging in my sweatshirt pocket for the orange bottle.

"Here's some water," he says passing back a water bottle.

I seen it's had some sips already taken. Most days I'd just pass the thing right back. I don't share spit with anyone except Sonia and even still I don't think I'd drink outa her water. I pop open the pill bottle and fish one out.

I look at it. It is big. It is a big pill.

I'd probably choke taking it dry.

Uncle Luis looks over his shoulder. "Go ahead," he says.

In one quick move the thing is down with a swig a his water and I hand the bottle back. "Thanks," I say.

We had this long day at the beach where we played like fools. It was so hot that we ended up getting wet, though none a us know how to swim. We killed each other with water though, getting it up in each other's faces and laughing like junkies. After a while we just sat on the shore and let the sun bake us dry. I think they might a fell asleep but I was stuck listening to the whoosh, whoosh sound a the waves talking. They be saying "Be Still, Be Still" as they're unrolling on the sand. And so that's just what we did. I think then maybe I got a little bit a this peace idea. I'm thinking it might be when you're not feeling scared or looking for trouble coming at you. It's when you just are. I also got a better mind on why people think it's so great.

"You ready?" Uncle Luis asks, because they already in the car and I'm just standing there like a boxhead staring at the sea.

"Yeah, sure," I say opening the back door.

"Sit up here," Kia says, and I see she already sitting in the middle a the front seat waiting for me.

I close the back door and get in the front. Phantom crawls into my lap and I put my hand over his head and down his back. He turns on the purr machine.

Since Kia said about getting her blood I haven't sat right next to her. Not like I'm scared a the blood or anything. It's more like a respect thing. Like she's a mini-woman now and I have to show her more respect.

It feels good to be up here though. I feel the sun coming off her skin and my clothes is still not dry for total so it feels good.

The sky is getting dim now without the strong sun and I look out over the water at all the colors there as we drive away.

"I thought we'd come back after dinner and see if we could get ourselves a look at some stars. What do you think?" Uncle Luis asks.

"Really?" Kia sounds happy surprised.

"Really," he tells her. "What do you think Edgar?"

"You alright with that?" I ask knowing he be afraid a the dark.

He nods. "Looking forward to it."

"Alright," I agree.

"Let's get ourselves some dinner and get changed and get back here then," he says.

I think this might be the best night a my whole life.

Chapter 22
North Carolina

I think this might be the best night of their whole lives, and I have just the slightest feeling of what it must be on a Christmas morning to see people you love get things they want or didn't know they wanted, but love. They have no idea what I have planned, but are about to unwrap it.

Earlier I was sitting in the Tidy Time Laundromat watching the machines spin around and around thinking this trip is so different than I imagined it. There's something about the rhythm of those machines that put me in a trance of sorts, where time was elastic and my thoughts were like bubbles above my head.

I looked at each of the kids. Kianna was sitting up on one of the machines swinging her feet and blowing bubbles with her pink gum, writing in her diary with a purple gel pen. Edgar was down the row of chairs with the cat on his lap using a sock to play with it. Then I saw there was something different about him and it took me a minute, but then I got it. His chains were off.

Looking back and forth between the two of them in my trance, I thought I could see something of their true nature, something I hadn't ever seen so clearly before. They have both changed so much in the past few days, and something is emerging. I thought if I sat in that state I might know what it was.

After a while of this, the machine right near me buzzed and the sound was like pushing the Total button after a long calculation. I realized it wasn't their changes that allowed me to see them, it was my own.

"Switch the clothes into the dryer," I said, putting the quarters into Kianna's hand. "I'm going to get some stuff next door. You two wait here."

Now maybe after all the running off these two had done already that would seem like a bad idea, but the buzzer was fresh in my head and I knew what I had to do.

And they were both there when I got back. Kianna was holding the cat and Edgar was doing chin-ups on a bar across the doorway. His side must be feeling better with the antibiotics. The dryers had less than five minutes to go. My timing was perfect. I had made my phone calls, gone to the grocery, the goodwill, and the bookstore. The goodwill had been a bonus because it was right next to the bookstore. I found thick wool army blankets there and some makeshift things for the cat— a couple of bowls and a bin we could make into a litter box.

It was a near perfect day at the beach, with only the slightest breeze. I had waited to bring up the idea of sleeping on the beach until I saw if they liked it. Neither of them had ever been to a beach, so I didn't know how it was going to go over. I wasn't surprised they loved it. I was only surprised how much they loved it. And that they both let themselves have fun, even after everything that has gone on during the trip.

It got hot after a while and they wanted to go in the water. At first I was concerned about Edgar getting his side wet and with Kianna menstruating. But then I just said it plain and they each said their part. Kianna said right out that it was done and I felt oddly relieved to hear that. Then Edgar pulled up his shirt and eased back the bandage to show the cut was healing fine. This surprised me because he has been so private. It also surprised me that he even wanted to get wet; he hates getting wet.

"All right, but keep the bandage on and put a dry one on after you're done," I said, sounding cautious to my own ears. I'm not used to sounding cautious. It used to be that I had everything organized so well that I knew just what was next. I didn't have to make any spontaneous decisions, never mind making them every five minutes. Now I'm flexing an unused muscle and I'm aware of the results of some of those un-thought-out decisions, like getting off the highway unexpectedly in New York City. That decision cost me getting shot at, losing the rear window of the car, nearly losing Edgar, and Edgar getting that cut. There seems to be an art to this spontaneous decision-making business, one I haven't yet figured out.

But I let the kids get wet, and I even got wet myself lifeguarding. It turned out to be one of the most fun days I have had in a long, long time. I suppose that good decision in some way balances out the bad decision of New York. Maybe it worked out better because we stopped and talked about it before we did it and so we all knew the risks and what we had to watch out for.

Now we're driving back out to the beach with full bellies, dry clothes, and a sunset waiting for us. The kids still don't know about the sleepout or the bag of marshmallows in the trunk.

Edgar is in the back looking at the astronomy book I got him at the bookstore. He's holding it real close to his face.

"Is it getting too dark to see?" I ask.

"Not too bad," he says.

"What do you say we build a fire on the beach?" I suggest.

"Yeah!" Kianna shouts.

Her voice startles the cat lying between us and he jumps. She reaches out and pets him back down. I haven't had a cat in a while. Jackson had one that adopted me when we lived together, and when I moved out I missed him terribly. Almost more than Jackson. Mr. T was his name. He was a gray and white with a long, dignified tail.

"Let's go to the same place we were today," Kianna says.

"If I can find it," I say.

"It's right down there," Edgar says, having looked up from his book.

"How do you know that?" Kianna challenges him, but he's right. I remember the parking spot had an oil spill stain in it that was shaped like Florida.

Edgar shrugs, confident, and goes back for one last look in his book.

"You're right!" Kianna shouts, having flung open the door and run to see if her sandcastle was still there.

The tide is high, but going out which is good for our sleepout plans.

Kianna begins to hunt for sticks while Edgar and I dig out a fire pit and collect big rocks for the outer edge. We don't say much while we work, but there is a rhythm to what we are doing that is a communication of its own. I'll have two big rocks in my hands and Edgar will move in without a word and dig out a space for them so they fit in perfectly next to the ones he put down. Then he'll get two more while I settle mine in and I'll do the same for him, based on the size rocks he's holding. Together, in this way, we make our fire pit.

What I like about Edgar is that he doesn't complain. He takes on what has to be done and does it without a lot of whining or trying to get out of it. And he's very good with his hands, and with how things fit.

We stand and admire our work as Kianna comes with another armload of sticks.

"Is that enough?" she asks.

I smile at Edgar. "Sure, that's fine. We can get more later."

Kianna has fallen asleep in my lap. Edgar is poking the fire with his marshmallow stick, sending a spray of red sparks into the night sky.

"You will have this all the time when you live in Miami with your grandmother," I say quietly, gesturing towards the ocean.

He doesn't say anything for a long time, and I think he is considering this, but then I realize he's figuring out how to say what he wants to say.

"It's not the only thing I want," he says.

"What else do you want?" I ask, not sure what he means.

"Sonia," he says right away.

"Who's Sonia?" I ask.

"My girl," he says, fishing something out. "This here's a charm she gave me off her bracelet before we left.

I take the small thing in my hand and hold it towards the firelight. It is a small silver charm in the shape of a full moon with the crescent moon raised along the edge. I just stare at it with the fire glowing behind. Edgar has held onto something for this whole time, concealed it, cherished it.

"It's nice," I say holding it up. "Do you love her?"

"Yeah," he says, not even hesitating.

He pokes the fire again and a new spray of sparks lift off. I shift Kianna in my lap so I can stretch out my legs.

"You got anyone you love?" he asks. And I understand the gesture he is making, but I'm not sure I'm ready.

"A couple people," I say, hugging Kianna to me.

Then he looks right at me. "I mean love love."

I cannot dodge his direct attempt to talk about this, and yet I feel a certain fear. It is how I felt when I was his age and talking about it meant ridicule or physical pain. How is it that I, a grown man, could be intimidated and ashamed here with this fourteen-year-old boy?

I clear my throat. "Not right now."

"You ever?"

"Yes." I hand him back his charm.

"Who was it?"

"A man named Jackson."

I'm not in the habit of talking about my love life with anyone, never mind my homophobic, adolescent nephew. My face breaks out in a sweat and my hands feel numb.

"How did you meet?" he asks and I can't believe he's going on with this.

I look up at the endless stars listed on the spreadsheet of sky and let the night air come into me in a long, slow breath. I have been holding it. I have been holding my breath intimidated and afraid of showing up completely, but this trip has been about risks and figuring out how to make spontaneous decisions, so I begin to tell him all of it.

"We met at a meeting," I say, and then I tell him the whole story backwards and forwards, looping around to my father and how he struck me across my face, about leaving my home, how I felt so alone and small. "If it weren't for your mother, I'm not sure what I would've done. She was so sure of herself and so sure of what to do next."

"Then why did she kill herself with drugs?"

When he asks this it is not with anger in his voice, but as if he really wants to know.

A spark pops out of the fire and, using the stick he's been poking it with, he pushes the lit piece into the sand.

"Your mother was an amazing person. You should never doubt that, but she fell into things on the street. We both did," I admit.

"You did?" He sounds genuinely shocked now.

"Is that so hard to believe?" I ask.

"Yes," he answers without hesitation and we both laugh.

My status has oddly gone up over this and even though it feels good for a moment, I can't live with him glorifying life on the street.

"It was the worst, most confusing part of my life," I say quietly.

Edgar is fingering the charm and doesn't look up. I want to warn him, to keep him from the pain and suffering of that life, but instead I let my head fall back to the stars. "Which one of these stars were you reading about?"

"I was learning about something called the summer triangle that comes out in May. Them three stars, Deneb, Vega, and Altair are the ones in it."

I'm impressed. "Do you know where they are up there?" I say, keeping my head tilted back at the view.

"I saw Vega right after we finished the fire pit. It's the first one to come out. Then I seen the other two bout when Kia fell asleep."

The secret life of Edgar Santiago is coming unveiled. "Where are they?" I ask and he goes on to patiently point each one out, telling me details from the astronomy book. This is by far the longest conversation I have ever had with my nephew and I continue to be surprised at each turn.

After a bit we both get quiet, inspecting the great galaxy. I'm still looking for where the river of the Milky Way breaks in two. His eyes are like telescopes and mine are like olives.

"How'd you get straight?" he asks, and I know he means off the drugs.

I let a pause in before I answer. Then I look over at him "I came here, to the ocean, to work a real job, met people who saw me differently then I saw myself. Back in Springfield I kept going to meetings to stay clean, and that's where I met Jackson."

"He a doper too?"

"No," I laugh, a little embarrassed. "He was leading the group."

I can't tell what he's thinking now, fingering the charm from his girl back home and looking at more stars than grains of sand beneath us, but his face looks peaceful enough.

"What happened to you two?" he asks.

Of all the questions he's asked on this subject, I find this one unexpectedly difficult to answer.

"What? Did you mess up?" he asks when I don't answer.

And I realize that is exactly what happened, only not how he thinks. "I guess I got scared," I admit.

"Hmmm…" he says, still moving the charm around between his fingers. "Think you ain't good enough," he says rather than asks, giving me more to think about.

Kianna turns a bit and stretches her arm out so that her hand lightly touches the sand. "I better lie her down," I say, shifting her in my lap. You want to sleep out here tonight?" I ask.

"For real?" he asks.

"For real. I got some blankets in the trunk." I dig into my pocket and throw him the keys. "What about the cat, though?" I ask.

"He can sleep with me," he says.

"Think he'll run off?"

"Nah, he's a scaredy cat."

Edgar leaves the light of the fire in the direction of the car while I lie Kianna down. She wakes briefly but then, tired out from the day, she falls quickly back to sleep. Edgar returns with the cat and the blankets and I spread a blanket across her.

"What about the fire?" he asks.

"Let's build it up some so it will keep us warmer longer."

After that we lie down on either side of Kianna. I spread the other blankets out over the three of us and settle in on my back.

The sky is amazing.

"Orion's belt. Is that the one just there?" I ask, pointing.

"Yup."

We are quiet a while, though I can sense that our conversation is not over.

"How did you know that you were like that?" he asks.

"I guess I always knew," I answer, knowing right where we are in the discussion.

"Did you want to kill yourself?"

"At times," I answer honestly.

In the quiet I can hear the waves, small now, as the tide recedes. I take a breath of the sea air and let it out slowly.

"Is there anything good about it?" he asks real softly.

"What do you mean?"

"I mean, you get beat up and called faggot, kicked out by your family. Is there anything good?"

"There's you," I say.

"What about me?" he says.

"If those things hadn't happened I wouldn't be here right now with you." I look into the night. "If you change even one thing in the past, then the present would be different. I am here right now because of all the circumstances of my life."

The sand is still warm from the day under my back, and the sky is limitless.

"I never thought about being a parent or taking responsibility for anyone. It didn't actually seem that good." A breeze touches my face. "But it is. And I never would've known that."

My mind turns to the journey we have taken this week, all the places I have been, all the feelings I have had that I've never had before. I think taking on kids might be a quicker way to learn about myself than entire box sets of cassettes.

Long after I think Edgar is asleep he says, "Geocentric theory."

I turn and look at his profile. He is staring up at the heavens and I can see his eyes are still wide open. It is like he is breathing in the view through his eyes. He is thinking in star language.

"What's geocentric theory?"

"That's what scientists thought was true, that earth was the center of the universe," he says. He is quiet again while the fire pops its last.

I settle my body into the sand and pull the blanket up over Kianna and under my chin.

My eyes are closing when I hear him. "Sometimes things ain't how they seem."

Chapter 23
North Carolina

Sometimes things aren't how they seem. This is the way it is a lot in dreams that a store can turn into a bird's nest.

I was just having this dream where there was no talking. Instead there was this real nice music playing. I was in the apartment in Springfield and it had the big Lincoln stained-glass window in it, real normal like it were any window. Edgar crawled in from the fire escape holding Phantom and waving the unfolded map. Uncle Luis came in holding his glasses and rubbing his eyes and behind him came the bald man from the gas station in Harlem. I guess they were boyfriends but again, in the dream it was real normal to me and Edgar like it weren't a big deal. Then it changed and we were in a hotel with blue shag carpet only the stained-glass window was still part of the room. I looked down off the couch like it was water instead of a rug, and then it was. I caught some on my foot to splash Edgar and the water went spraying through the air real slow and pretty where I could see each separate drop.

That's when Edgar turns over and knocks me awake.

The dream feeling was thick and stayed with me though until I opened my eyes. I could see the sliver of the moon dangling real low in the sky like a hangnail. That's when I remembered that we were on this trip with Uncle Luis and that we were sleeping out on the beach. The water was making its in and out sound and the sky was still real clear and my favorite blue black color. I tried to remember the poem I wrote in my diary yesterday about the sea, but it wouldn't come to me.

So I reached under the blanket and took out the Good Shepherd card I'd slid into my back pocket last night when we changed into dry clothes. I'd been using it as a bookmark for the book Uncle Luis bought me about a girl who gets her period. But I finished it when I was waiting for them to come out, and my backpack was in the car, so I just slipped the card into my back pocket. I'm glad I did though, because then I had it to take out.

I just stared a long time at the face of Jesus and the face of the lamb. For some reason it made me think of Edgar holding Phantom, though they didn't look a thing alike. Still, something about the feeling was the same. There's a feeling they're related. I thought then that if Jesus could be related to a lamb, that maybe I could still be related to Edgar and Luis. Related in that feeling way.

Now I'm lying here thinking of last night and how we ate and changed into warm clothes and came out here to the beach so Edgar could have his first real look at his stars. He had his new book from Uncle Luis and the two of them made a fire so they could see the pages. I went along the dunes to collect sticks and instead of feeling scared or lonely I felt just right. My fleece sweat-shirt felt hot then so I tied it around my waist for later. I'm glad I have it now though because it's a little cold with the fire burnt out.

Momi bought me this fleece for a surprise, no reason, not my birthday or anything, just because. I can see her face watching me when I took it out the bag and held it up.

"Do you like it?" she asked.

She asked this because it's not what you'd call my color. It's like a funny green, like mint ice cream. Honestly I didn't know at first if I liked it or not, even though I smiled then and told her I did. But now it's like one of my favorite things I got. The color was something I had to grow into I guess.

Thinking of Momi is hurting a little less, though I wish I hadn't lost that picture a her.

Last night I didn't think any of that about the fleece. I was too excited about the fire.... I never made a fire before. Never saw one shoot up and thought it a good thing. At first I had a bad feeling that fires bring on in me. I remember seeing one down our block in an apartment and though Momi kept shushing me I couldn't help crying as we watched.

Then there was the fire in the bathroom at our school that everyone thought Edgar lit, but I knew it wasn't true. I was down the hall in Miss Munoz's class then and Edgar was in Ms. L's room right near the bathroom that got lit up, so maybe that's why they thought it was him. Ms. L knew it wasn't him though. That's why I prayed the whole night before I moved classes that I'd be put in hers. It paid off and I got put in hers this year and thought I was gonna get to stay in there for three whole years. I wish I could talk to Ms. L right now and tell her I got my bleeding all done. She's white with that straight blonde hair, but she don't act like it. She's like a arrow she's so right on a topic, anything kids pitch to her she pitches it right back, so it wouldn't be a problem for me to talk to her about it. Thinking about fires makes all kinds of stuff come into your brain.

Last night though, I just kept saying to myself that this one was good and it wasn't going to do any harm and after a while the bad feelings went away. It might have been when Uncle Luis brought out them marshmallows and showed us how to poke them on the end of one a the sticks I collected, and then we set them over the lower flames. They turned all brown on the outside, though Edgar's caught on fire and burnt up black. Then Uncle Luis pulled it onto some square cookie with a bit a chocolate and it plopped there all soft and gooey. He took another cookie and mushed it down on top to make the best sandwich I ever tasted.

The sound a the waves, with all the stars and the sweet taste in my mouth brought on such a state that I hugged Uncle Luis till we fell over in the sand. He laughed and then pulled me into his lap and we sat like that for a real long time watching the fire. I figure it was dark enough not to matter that I'm not a little kid anymore. Anyway, it was cooling off and I put on my fleece and it felt real good there.

That's when I told Uncle Luis that I want to go home. It just kinda popped out unexpected, but it is true enough. I'm tired of moving from place to place. I want to stop now.

It was real good though, because no one said anything. We all just kept sitting there quiet. I was glad because I didn't say it to break the mood or make a big conversation. It was just the truth.

After that I musta fallen asleep in Uncle Luis's lap, because the next thing I know he's laying me down on the sand saying, "We're going to sleep here tonight."

"What about Phantom?" I mumbled to him.

"Edgar's taking care of him," he said quiet.

Then I fell into a real deep sleep, until that dream.

The sky is starting to grow light and I turn so I can try to find where the sun will be coming into the picture. Then I see something worth waking everybody up to see.

"Edgar," I say shaking him on the shoulder careful not to hurt his side. I reach on my other side. "Uncle Luis, wake up."

They both mutter and turn.

"Look," I say.

And after a minute or two, they do.

On one side of us the little crescent, like God's cupped hand to his ear, is hanging in the sky over the dunes. Then looking the other way, over the water is the edge of the sun starting to burst. The sky on that side is covered in colors I've never seen in the air before. There are all sorts a oranges and pinks and the sun itself is this hot red. The water is doing this cool mirror thing so there are colors on colors on colors. Then turning back to the moon, the sky is all cool blues, darks and lights with the whole of the moon showing just slight behind the silver part.

None of us say a word. We just sit there looking from one sky to the other, one way of the sky to another way. It's like a show that goes on for a long time and we just sit there staring.

When the sun is yellow and more regular, like I'm used to seeing it, Uncle Luis clears his throat.

At first I think he's going to say something important, but then he doesn't.

"What do you say we get on the road?"

I look at him. His glasses are off, his face has all stubble on it, and his shirt is wrinkled so as he looks like somebody I've never seen before.

"Get on the road?" I ask.

He looks over to Edgar then, who's holding Phantom on his lap.

"Yes," Uncle Luis says. "If you're ready?"

I don't really want to get up from this warm place between these two where I feel just right. But I take in a deep, deep sniff a the sea, big enough to fill me up and live in me for a while yet.

"I'm ready," I say looking at the sun up with the light bouncing crazy off the water.

Epilogue
One year later

When I told her she was right about holding out for miracles her black face lit up and she was smiling so wide her teeth were like the sparkling edge of the ocean with the light bouncing crazy off the water. I can say things like that now that I been there. I think actually that's where the miracle caught up with us. Anyway, she said of course she'd come and now I'm waiting on this wood bench scuffing the floor with my new shoes. They're so shiny I can see my face in them and I give a grin to myself, crooked tooth and all—that's the kinda day it is today.

Uncle Luis is so nervous I thought he was gonna pee hisself, but now he's in the bathroom "freshening up" so I don't have to worry about that anymore. It's weird to be here by myself waiting for everybody, but there was a big line at the door for security when we come so I guess everybody else got stuck in that too. Good thing Edgar took off them stupid gold chains or he never woulda made it through the metal detector we all gotta go through. Now he wears a shark tooth Uncle Luis bought him in North Carolina the day we made our plan.

We planned it all out on a napkin the morning after we slept out on the beach and it's happening just like we said. Well, not exactly like we said because we didn't know the car would up and die ten miles outside of Springfield and we'd have to get towed home. We laughed, relieved we decided not to go to Miami, but to use the money for a plane ticket instead. Then we'd a been stuck in Miami instead of back home. It's turning out to be a good thing that the car died anyway because a couple months ago Uncle Luis and Edgar decided to fix it up themselves for when Edgar learns to drive figuring they got no rush since it's still a year away. Edgar's real good with his hands though and I heard the engine catch in the back alley this morning when I was getting out the shower, so I know it's coming along.

We live with Uncle Luis right near the library and he last fall he got us both cards so we can get books whenever we want. I thought Edgar would never use his, but right away he got out books on stars and galaxies. Then when they decided to fix up the car he got a couple "How To" books about cars, and sure enough it must be helping.

I was sad last summer thinking we were going to have to move away from the library when we got our new apartment big enough for all of us. Turned out Uncle Luis's old boyfriend's therapy office is next to a Real Estate one, and he heard right off when another, bigger apartment in our same building came up and he got it for us like that. It seems that made something better between him and Uncle Luis because then he started coming around a lot and they both had that look. Pretty soon it's the new school year and Jackson's comin along to back-to-school night. I don't care none though cause I always liked Jackson anyway. He looks like a tall, bald version of Miss Faith, and Ms. L don't care who your people are, she's just glad when people come.

"Edgar!" I jump up and wave and I don't mind that it looks stupid. Edgar's coming down the hall holding Sonia's hand and they look beautiful. He's got a haircut and his glasses look real sharp with the shirt and tie he picked out with Uncle Luis. That was on the napkin— that we'd all go shopping and get new clothes for the big day. I didn't expect Sonia to look like that though. She's got new cornrows in her hair with yellow and orange beads at the end—not plastic ones—breakable ones with little white flecks. Her face has got makeup on it, but real light, not like Xoshell who makes it look like a Halloween costume, and her dress is light, light yellow with no sleeves at all.

I think maybe Sonia saved Edgar's life 'cause she was the reason he finally agreed to do eighth grade over this year. When Uncle Luis first talked to him about it I thought he was going to leave us for true and go back to them guys on the street he wasn't hanging with any-more. But Uncle Luis turned out to be smart about Edgar and he did it with Miss Faith, who can talk a cat into a swimming pool. They told him it would be a year to make up for all the things he lost because of everything that happened and that he could go to High School pre-pared. Uncle Luis had already started playing chess with him then, which they still do practically every night, and I guess he used a bunch a examples from that to explain why it was a good idea. Everybody knows the final thing though was that Sonia was in seventh grade and he was going to have to leave her, so if he stayed at Zanetti again he would be with her. That and they hired a new middle school teacher.

Now Edgar can read as good as me even though I'm reading a lot of books. Uncle Luis says to be a story writer you've got to read a lot of people's stories and see all the ways they tell it. Sometimes when I read a real good one I think I'll never be able to do it that beautiful or that strong. But then I open up my new journal and write a new one anyway. Sometimes I cheat and add a word I learned from somebody else's story, but Ms. L says that's not cheating, that's learning. She was the one who also explained right away when we got back last year that I was going to get my period again and again. At the time I remember my head dropped and I felt real discouraged, but she lifted my chin up with her hand and looked right in my eyes. Her big blue eyes was sparkly as treasure and then it was fine. I guess that's what I was waiting for all along, someone to see the change in me.

Sonia hugs me and her arms with no sleeves makes me think of that real hot day last year when we left and how miserable I was and how I had no idea all that was gonna happen after that. Maybe soon I'll be remembering today in the city courthouse standing in my shiny shoes thinking I had no idea all that was gonna come next. Maybe that will just keep happening.

"Kianna." Uncle Luis has come up behind me from the bathroom and he's wrestling with his red tie.

He had to tie both him and Edgar this morning and now his needs fixing in the worst way. "Have you seen Jackson yet?" he asks as he bends down so I can reach it and I wish I'd paid closer attention to all the loops he was making.

I shake my head no as I take the smooth red silk in my hands. It feels like hand lotion slipping over my fingers it's so fine. He didn't say he picked this one cause of all that happened, but the color sure reminds me of our trip, the red car, the red sun rising.

Maybe he knows I got no idea what I'm doing with the tie because he doesn't seem annoyed at all when it's knotted up funny. He just says "thank you" and looks at me for a second longer than usual.

"Have you seen Jackson?" Uncle Luis asks Edgar who's looking moony at Sonia.

"Nah," Edgar starts to answer.

"No. The word is no, not nah," Uncle Luis starts cause a his nerves.

Lucky because of Ms. L, I got into peer mediation this year, so I learned some stuff to help it not be a problem. Miss Faith has some fancy name for it, but I just think it's talking good sense.

"Uncle Luis," I say sweetly. "I'm thinking this isn't the best time for working on our talking." I take special care to say isn't instead of ain't here.

Right away he smiles. "You're right. Sorry, Edgar. You look wonderful. You both look wonderful." He hugs Sonia while he's babbling. Edgar looks at me while he does it, and we both be grinning. We've had a whole year to figure Uncle Luis out, and we got it pretty good now. It's even helping Edgar with his temper cause Uncle Luis is so quick to say when he messes up Edgar doesn't have time to get mad.

When I turn around everybody is here now and it's one big greeting party. Miss Faith is hugging Sonia, Uncle Luis is greeting Ms. L, and Father Brown is there shaking hands with Edgar while Mrs. Perez talks to them loud in Spanish—too loud and I want to shush her, but instead I laugh.

Then I see something that catches my laugh up in my throat. I feel Uncle Luis's hand on my shoulder and I know he's seen too. Then Edgar must see us looking 'cause he looks and Mrs. Perez stops talking and the hall goes total quiet.

Slow down the hall comes Jackson and on his arm is the stooped old woman that must be my grandmother. This is the part of the napkin I didn't think would happen, that she would use the ticket we sent her and fly from Miami to Springfield to say Uncle Luis could take us for legal. My heart is speeding up and slowing down so that I don't know what's going on with it flopping around inside my chest. I have to lean against Uncle Luis. He must feel something similar 'cause he leans on me too and puts both his arms around the front of me holding me to him. I don't see him coming but then there's Edgar with his hands on us both propping us up so we all three are in some kinda big lean.

I guess seeing a miracle can make you feel faint, make you awful glad you have people to lean up on when your heart is bursting out making a new galaxy.

Acknowledgments

This book would not exist without the consistent encouragement of my writing group, the Fairview Writers: Elissa Alford, Margaret Babbott, Amy Dryansky, Maya Janson, Mary Koncel, and Sarah Metzer, who helped me figure out pages-a-day.

Nor would it be what it is without the honest critique of my Spalding Novel Workshop participants: Dave Degoyer, Karen Mann, Susan Masters, Jennifer Sherlock, and John Steele, under the perceptive guidance of Kenny Cook. Their insights brought shape and cohesion to the journey.

I'm indebted to my editors, JL Evans and Jean Zimmer, for the careful fine-tuning that really got the engine humming. Also to my readers, Kenny Cook and Dena Salmon, who offered new perspectives on the book as a whole and whose kind words were fuel for my engine.

Finally, this book would not be in print were it not for the persistence of Jasper Price-Slade, who prayed nightly for it to be published. His confidence in the outcome gave me license to drive it out of revisions, through every rest stop, clear to publication.

Author's Note

This is a work of the imagination, inspired by my time at the Zanetti Montessori School in Springfield, Massachusetts. Zanetti was the first public Montessori program in all of western Massachusetts and was developed as a Magnet program to convert the school that held some of the lowest test scores and the highest incidents of violence in the district into a Montessori school. Shortly following the implementation of the Montessori program those statistics changed.

Though this story begins in a real school, in its original location on Howard Street, the characters are works of fiction. The teachers and students of that school, at that time, breathe life into these invented characters, for we all share a common story—one of disconnection, connection, loss, joy, longing, confusion, clarity, and the sense of being on a quest. It is a story about finding and claiming home, and through this story I express my gratitude for having found home there.